Critical acclaim for *(un)arranged marriage*:

'Absorbing and engaging written from a male poin debut from Bali Rai th will identify

'A story that confronts controversial issues head-on and yet manages to be a very entertaining novel'
The Bookseller

'Energetically and pacily written ... There is a vitality and freshness about Rai's writing that engages the reader ... An intriguing debut that promises well for the future' *Books for Keeps*

'Readers of this excellent book from a promising new writer will not be disappointed' *Kids Out*

'Rai has an unselfconscious style, and a dry sense of the ridiculous ... an appealing subversive edge' *TES*

'Any teenager under pressure from his or her parents to conform will enjoy this novel' *Guardian*

**Also available by Bali Rai,
and published by Corgi Books:**

(un)arranged marriage

*Winner of the Angus Book Award
Winner of the Leicester Book of the Year Award
Winner of the Stockport Schools Award
Shortlisted for the Lancashire Children's
Book Award, the North East Book Award,
the South Lanarkshire Book Award,
Wirral Paperback of the Year and the Branford Boase Award*

the crew

bali rai

CORGI BOOKS

THE CREW
A CORGI BOOK 978 0 552 54739 0
First published in Great Britain by Corgi Books,
an imprint of Random House Children's Books

Corgi edition published 2003

5 7 9 10 8 6

The Random House Group Limited makes every effort to ensure that the papers used in
its books are made from trees that have been legally sourced from well-managed and
credibly certified forests. Our paper procurement policy can be found at:
www.randomhouse.co.uk/paper.htm

Set in 12/14½ Bembo MT Schoolbook by
Falcon Oast Graphic Art Ltd.

Corgi Books are published by Random House Children's Books,
61-63 Uxbridge Road, London W5 5SA,
A Random House Group Company.

Addresses for companies within The Random House Group Limited can be found at:
www.randomhouse.co.uk/offices.htm

THE RANDOM HOUSE GROUP Limited Reg. No. 954009

www.kidsatrandomhouse.co.uk

A CIP catalogue record for this book is available from the British Library.

Printed in the UK by CPI Bookmarque, Croydon, CR0 4TD

A big thank you to Penny and Jennifer Luithlen,
and everyone at Random House.

To all the schools, pupils and librarians who voted for
me in various awards, especially everyone at Angus,
Stockport and the Leicester Book Award. And extra-special
thanks to the K. Blundell Trust for their support.

To all the pupils in schools around the country
who tell me what they'd like to read.

Once again, to my sister Avi and Jes, her husband,
and my mum, for their continued support – big love.

To my friends Jeff, Parmy, Ben, Anna and everyone else –
for their encouragement. Nice one.

Thanks to Mick, Julia and Christopher Sykes,
and to Jane Sykes for being my best girl.

A big kiss to Jasmine for the website, the opinions
and the conversations.

And finally, to Irene, Kate and Nancy and the
whole Dooher clan – with the most love;
and for Fran 'Smiler' Dooher – I miss you. R.I.P.

one:

the crew

Ellie is the youngest. She's fourteen and she tagged on to me about a year ago after moving to the ghetto from somewhere down south. Her family moved in next door to me but I never spoke to her until I saw her on the ring road that circles the very edge of the city centre – a concrete merry-go-round that separates one part of the ghetto from another.

A couple of youths were chatting her up, eyeing up her mobile phone. They were both older than her – fifteen – and looking to raise a little cash by mugging her. She just thought they were being nice. I watched them from across the road as they reeled her in like some kind of prize-winning prey and, just as one of them made his move, I darted across the merry-go-round, dodging a red Beamer by the width of my thigh, and bounced him down onto the broken concrete pavement with a shoulder barge. The other one made a grab for Ellie's phone and bag – only to feel the full force of one of her feet down his shin and onto his foot. He cried out, cussed her and then, turning to find me staring at him, decided to do a runner. Ellie pulled out her house keys, calling me names that fourteen-year-old girls on TV don't use. I dodged one lunge from her, and another, then grabbed her round her shoulders with a bear hug, telling her to chill out. I was a friend, I told her. I lived next door. She made to break away a couple of times before she stopped wriggling. And then she started crying.

Ellie never leaves the house without matching the colour of her mobile phone cover, her top and the piping on her trainers. She has three colours at the moment – pink, yellow and blue. I used to laugh at her but it's one of her little 'things' and her trainers are always wicked. Besides, as a man, what do I know about fashion? At least that's what she always tells me.

She has blonde hair and a really pretty baby-face with bright blue eyes that haven't changed much since she was about five, if her dad's photo album is anything to go by. It's why we call her Baby. Some of the other girls round here don't like her and call her 'Stush' and other stupid names because they don't know her and think she's stuck up. The Crew looks after her, though. We don't do business with racism and jealousy and all that. Positive attitudes only. And we look after each other. You mess with one of us – then you have to deal with us all.

Jas is older – sixteen, like me. He lives across the street with his mum. A Punjabi, he's got this really fiery temper that gets him into trouble with some of the older crews round here. His mum is a rarity in that she is an Asian single mum. His dad used to beat her up until, after years of abuse, she left him when Jas was nine. When his parents then got divorced, it was like a major problem for his extended family. Divorce, according to them, brings shame on the family and Jas and his mum get all sorts of shit from them. They totally ignored the violence of his dad – like that stuff is OK as long as the neighbours, the police and the social workers don't find out. How messed up is that, man? One of his uncles drives a taxi round here and told Jas's grandparents that their daughter was working the streets, just because he saw her walking home with a black man. That caused some real problems but his mum just ignored it all and got on with being a nurse, which is what she does for a job. Oh, and Jas's mum cooks the best curry in the world.

Jas is nearly six feet tall already and he wears his hair in a fade. He's into hip-hop and skateboarding in his baggy, no-ass jeans and hooded tops. I met him in junior school and he protects the Crew, along with me and Will – if we ever need to. I'll tell you about Will later. Jas is a trained kick-boxer and he can handle himself if things ever hit critical. He's on the under-card for a world title fight. His coach is already the best fighter in Europe, and Jas is trying to get his club to take the whole Crew to the fight, which is in Manchester. That's what Jas wants to do. That and making hip-hop music of his own. He's cool.

Della is fifteen – sixteen next month – and she's *wild*. I met her years back when she was only nine, taxing some boys down the end of my street. One of her victims knew her and made a comment about her dad. He paid for it. Trainers, gold chain and two loose front teeth. She's been in care on and off for years and at the moment she lives with her latest and – she says – last foster-mum, Sue. She calls Sue her real mum. Her *only* mum. Della's dad got put in prison when she was eight. He was a pimp. Her mum died a year afterwards. Heroin. Della has grown up the hard way, especially as a young black girl, facing all

9

the negative stereotypes that the social 'services' have. At first they kept on farming her out to middle-class white couples in posh areas. She hated that. Not because her foster-families were white, but because she couldn't relate to them. I mean, Sue's white and Della really loves her. The difference is that Sue doesn't see Della as a problem teenager. Just a teenager with problems.

Della is about five eight with the figure of a grown woman. She wears cut-off tops and short skirts and stuff to show it off. Her hair is braided and sits just under her jaw line, and her eyes are kind of catlike, bright green in colour. She looks a lot like Lauryn Hill and most of the men round here try it on with her all the time. But they don't realize that Della is one tough sister. She is as hard as nails on the surface and can cause a man heart trouble when she stares, but on the inside she is softer and more vulnerable. She was wary of Ellie at first, thought she was an impostor. Now she treats Ellie like a little sister. She has a thing for Jas too, which she confided to me one night. I'm not supposed to even mention it, on pain of death. I believe her too.

Will is the same height as Jas but twice as wide. He lives in the next street with his mum and dad. His dad works part-time for the council as a landscape gardener and does building jobs for cash the rest of the time, while his mum used to be a dinner lady. She's housebound now with really bad arthritis and Will takes care of her a lot. His parents are Jamaican and he is really light-skinned with a big, friendly smile. People are still wary of him though because he's massive. Seventeen stone of pure muscle which he pounds into shape four days a week at the local Community Centre gym. And he can get well leery too. He doesn't like being told what to do and he hates people who try it on. He is more than capable of fighting his corner and around the ghetto that counts for a lot.

Will is sixteen too and he loves garage music and R & B. He wants to be a DJ and is trying to save up money from the cash-in-hand building jobs that he does with his old man. He's only got the one deck at the minute but he found an old mixer in a skip, which he took home and fixed up. Man, when he's listening to a garage mix you can't get him to speak, never mind get up off his big ass. He's my oldest friend – we met at infant school – and the Crew is his second family. That's how he sees us all. Believe me, at times it's like having a dad when he gets one on.

And then there's me. My name is Billy, although everyone calls me Sleepy. My mum called me that when I was a kid because I liked to sleep so much, and getting me out of my bed is kind of hard work even now. It's also the nickname of her favourite reggae artist, Horace Andy. My mum is Punjabi, like Jas's mum, and my dad, who I don't really know as I haven't seen him since I was a little kid, is Jamaican. I live with my mum and her boyfriend, Nanny, a Rastafarian. My mum was always skint before Nanny showed up and at one point she was a working girl, over by the church crossroads. I got loads of shit for that when I was younger but I love my mum and I respect how much she had to sacrifice to keep me in food and clothes. She works with abused and battered women now, including the girls who work the streets, and sometimes she cries about the past and gets moody. I always tell her she should hold her head up high. She's a

11

strong, independent woman, my mum, and nothing she ever did can change that.

One of the things that I missed out on by never seeing my dad as I grew up was learning to ride a bike, which I still can't do. It's one of my biggest secrets and it still embarrasses me. When I was twelve and thirteen everyone round here had bikes of some sort – mostly nicked ones – so I desperately wanted my own too, but instead of letting the other kids know about my shame, I just called them all losers and started nicking cars with some older lads. Joyriding cost me my school place and one of my best friends. It also upset my mum and Nanny, although if it hadn't been for their support and anger, I would have ended up doing time. I don't *blame* my dad for that. I made my own choices. I just wish he had been around.

I'm the same height as Della and I look Indian rather than Jamaican. Della reckons I'm too thin and need to put on a few pounds, but I like being the size I am and I can look after myself as well as anyone around me. Della also thinks that I have a soft spot for Ellie, which I suppose is true, and she teases me constantly. I'm like the unofficial leader of the Crew – but only because we use my bedroom as our HQ. We don't deal with real leaders – everyone gets a say because everyone is equal.

Everyone except Zeus, that is. Zeus is our mascot and has been ever since he turned up outside our house one night, bleeding badly from a gash to the head. He's a Rottweiler and he is the stupidest dog you've ever seen. All he does is lie on his paws, eat too much food and dribble. He's useless as a guard dog and we have to bribe him with Mars bars to get him out of the house for a walk. But he is an honorary part of the Crew and we all look after him, although he lives at my mum's or at Ellie's because none of the others have houses with gardens or yards.

two:

the ghetto

The ghetto is just a nickname for some of the estates round the city centre. They aren't like the ghettos you see on TV – like the ones in the USA or in the developing world (I used to call it the Third World until Nanny showed me what he calls the 'truths and rights': the world is one place – only some countries have more power than the rest). They are ghettos in an economic sense, though. Most of the people are skint all the time and there are certain alleys and streets where drug dealers stand around in the open and you can see all the addicts wandering about looking to get high. Every so often the police raid one or two of the drug houses and for a few nights afterwards the business moves elsewhere. But it always comes back. Always. One dealer just gets replaced by another because there are plenty of kids around here looking to step up their station in life and crime is usually the only way they can do that. Not the Crew, though. We don't deal with no hard drugs.

And then there's the working girls. You would probably call them prostitutes, I suppose, but I've been brought up to treat them as human beings and not criminals. My mum believes that they should be given legal worker status like in Holland and be able to leave the streets, where they get treated like shit by pimps and dealers. I totally agree with her too because all I've ever seen growing up is like this endless succession of screwed-up girls with drug habits on the corners around my neighbourhood. They look like baby gazelles on an African plain being eyed hungrily by leopards. Once me and Della met a fourteen-year-old girl down by the church. She asked Della if she had a fag and I could see the bruises on her arms and legs. I wanted to take her to see my mum but she refused. Eventually Della and I left her where she was and on the way home Della had tears running down her cheeks. We spent hours at my house talking about how messed up the world was. At one point Nanny came into my room and started talking about Babylon – his name for the capitalist system – and how it was this great big trap, duping the people into believing that material wealth was the only goal worth living for.

'Nuff man don't see the truth until it too late, man. No education, except brainwashing. No real chance ina life. Heads of government nah care and the people dem stay hungry. That's Babylon, man.'

After a while he lost me and Della, and he went off to catch 'a lickle irie meditation'.

I hope I'm not painting too bad a picture of the area that we all live in. It isn't as bad as many people like to make out, but then it isn't exactly a garden full of roses either. Yeah, we get some really bad things happening around here. But, like Nanny is always telling me, positivity comes from within. Nanny's always got a wise old proverb to explain the world's problems – but more about him in a minute.

I love my area and the rest of the Crew do too. None of us are blind to the problems – for us they are just a part of life, like trees in the country or red buses in London. They are like local attractions, only more hazardous to your health. But as well as all the rubbish, there're also these little alleys that come off the streets, where people have planted herbs in window boxes and you can smell basil and coriander as you walk by. There're the big old houses named after Roman and Greek gods. Next door to my mum's house is *Apollo* and up the street we've got *Minerva*. The Romans made her the goddess of war and education as well as arts and crafts. Nanny told me that, before shaking his head and cussing the Romans for linking war with such positive pastimes. I just laughed at him. The kids round here have to go to war every day just to get an education and then fall at the entrance to uni because it costs too much money. I haven't told Nanny that one yet but I will one day.

Some of the streets are lined with trees, so it's not like a total concrete jungle. Some of the trees are actually green, too. And there is always something happening or someone around. Music thumps out of car stereos and through walls and windows day and night and the young kids see everything as one big adventure playground. I used to when I was a kid. The amount of fun you can have in a derelict house is unbelievable. The dealers and that leave you alone unless you are a punter or you get in their way during their 'runnin's'. In fact the most aggressive people around if you're a kid are the homeless drunks because they get territorial about their particular doorways and benches. I've seen so many kids running out of the little playground at the end of my street, being chased by some stumbling drunken old man with a yellow stained beard. The homeless and the drunks are just another part of our landscape.

Territory is important for the gangs too. Every two or three streets have their own little gang and most of the members are between the ages of nine and seventeen. Some of the gangs are exclusively black or Asian, but mostly they are mixed, with a few white kids thrown in too. Every so often there are street fights, although they aren't too serious most of the time. They tend to be little scuffles which get broken up by some irate parent caught in the middle. I've seen Nanny lecture two groups of youths about 'war in de ghetto' many a time. In fact, one time he took about sixteen young lads up to Victoria Park with a football and got them to settle their differences over an eight-a-side game. All the kids ended up as mates and they eventually formed an even bigger gang which Nanny got pissed off about. Man, I just laughed at him.

Around here you have to have a crew otherwise you get treated like an outsider and that is not a good position to be in, believe me. You need to have someone to watch your back – someone to go to when shit goes wrong. Most of us can't go to the police or our schoolteachers. Things don't work like that for us. We have to look out for each other. That's why the Crew got together and why we are so close now. No one has a go if they know you are part of a gang. Well, not regularly. It's the older gangs that cause all the real trouble. They can be really dangerous. Most of the older crews are in the streets dealing and mugging, like our local bad boy, Busta, who doesn't like me or any of the rest of the Crew. We tend to avoid him, if we can.

One of the older lads that I was knocking around with a while back, David, started out in one of those older gangs. He's the one who taught me how to break into cars and how to drive. Thing is, once he'd had enough of the cars he moved on to running errands for a local dealer and eventually he got so hooked up in all the heroin and speed he was dealing he didn't even look like the same person. He ended up robbing grannies and school kids in broad daylight and made his girlfriend work out by the church. She got taken into care and David overdosed in the back of an abandoned car down by the front line. He was eighteen when he died but everyone round here had seen it coming for years before it actually happened. Life can be kind of tough round here to begin with, but people like David stack the chips against themselves from day one.

As for me, I know that the easiest thing for me to do would be to just go with the flow and end up selling 't'ings' or robbing and that. But I ain't no sheep and no one round here is leading me. I'm going to lead myself. Straight out of here, if I have to. I don't know what I'm going to do yet. I wouldn't mind going back to college, only that costs money, something I ain't got. Thing is, not knowing what I want to do doesn't stop me from dreaming about escaping. I will, too, even though I don't really like the idea that I will probably have to leave my home area one day. I won't hesitate if it means I'm going to keep my freedom or my life. Like I keep saying: life around here is harsh, man.

However, little rays of sunshine do light up the concrete jungles. They break through the gloom of grey skies and never-ending problems. One of the biggest rays of sunshine in my life has been Nanny. He's been around since I was a little kid and he's the actual father that my real father never was. Nanny is like a best mate and a teacher rolled into one. He's about six feet tall and his dreadlocks reach halfway down his back. He's slim, but strong as an ox. He lifts free weights at home and goes jogging every morning. My mum has even got him doing yoga, although I think he does it just to keep her quiet. He's been with my mum since a few years after my old man left us, and she told me once that he was the reason she was able to stop being a working girl. Nanny shared all his money with her when she had it really hard after being arrested years back. We got evicted from our flat and he took us in, even though he only lived in a one-bedroom place in a high-rise. When my mum went through college and uni, it was Nanny who brought me up, making me breakfast and taking me to school and stuff. He used to make the dinner too, and do all the cleaning around the house, which is pretty much how things have stayed ever since. Nanny has never had what my teachers would call a 'proper job' ever, but he has his reasons.

Nanny is a Rastafarian. Not like the ones that you see stereotyped in Hollywood films, all high on crack and shooting people and shit. Nanny is a true Rasta. He doesn't eat meat or shellfish and never touches booze. The only tobacco he smokes is the hand-rolled stuff he uses to build spliffs, and you can't even use the word 'drugs' around him. Drugs, for Nanny, means things like crack and heroin. Alcohol, even. But not weed. He calls his weed a spiritual tool – one that helps him to meditate and achieve peace with the world around him. It's not like he smokes all day long either. Most times he smokes in the evenings, after he has done all his duties for the day.

Weed is the thing that frees his mind from the mental slavery of Babylon and I don't reckon it seriously harms him – or anyone else for that matter. I've seen men round here get beaten and cut up by drunks, but I've never seen anyone get angry after smoking a spliff.

I respect Nanny's beliefs. As a Rasta, he believes that Babylon is corrupt and he chooses not to participate in what he calls 'wage slavery' – having a job. Instead he sorts out a little weed for his mates, enough to get his own for free, and my mum shares her money with him. She calls it his 'wages' for the work he does around the house. Like housekeeping, I suppose. He's an electrician too, doing little jobs for the people we know as and when they need him. Nothing regimented. It's not like he is self-employed and that. He just fixes stuff for a small fee sometimes, or in exchange for things we need.

It might sound like a weird notion but I reckon his beliefs are just as valid as other views and I love to sit and discuss things with him. I don't necessarily agree with everything he believes in, like the idea of Haile Selassie as God but, at my age, I just want to be open to all sorts of ideas before I decide what I do and don't believe. I do see the Babylon system that Nanny talks about. I see it every day. The rich control the poor and the poor just follow like sheep. 'Mental slavery' is what Nanny calls it.

'Dem brainwash de yout', dem man. The yout' kill

each other jus' ta wear the criss trainers but dem don' realize is the trut' dem disconnect from. The trut', man.'

That's a typical piece of what Nanny calls his 'reasoning'. He knows loads of facts and figures which he uses to argue his point – stuff he has bothered to go and research down the library or on the Internet, although he's not the biggest fan of the Web. Says that it's too sinister when the government can see exactly what you are downloading. He thinks that they compile files on everyone or something – just from what they look at on the Net. He's like the ghetto professor and everyone knows him. Sometimes me and the rest of the Crew listen to him for hours.

three:

friday

'*That bloke was down the end of the alley again tonight.*'
I was telling Billy and Della, but they both looked at me
in the same way. As if to say '*What's Ellie on about now . . . ?*'
I looked straight at Billy and then, feeling myself starting to
blush, I looked away again. Sometimes I hate being the youngest
member of the Crew. I feel like I have to prove myself all the time
and I don't like that. So instead of continuing my story I started
to sulk — pouting, because I knew it wound the other two up. It
worked too. It always does.

'*Ellie, look, it's not like we don't believe you . . .*' started Billy.

'*But there are loads of other gardens that back onto that alley
and—*' That was Della.

'*—and maybe the bloke you keep seeing is just some new
neighbour,*' Billy finished the sentence off. I mean, what were
they? Twins?

I looked at them both in turn, pouting some more, but
eventually I relented — I could always put it on again later. If I
had to.

I wasn't lying to them. I don't do lies. Well, all right, maybe
tiny little white ones now and then. But not serious ones. I mean,
why would I lie to Billy or Della? They're my best friends.

Especially Billy. I ain't never told him how much I love him for rescuing me back when we met and introducing me to the rest of the Crew. I can't tell him. It's like whenever I think about it, I get all choked up and want to cry. And I'm not crying in front of him. Besides, he's a typical bloke — never says the right thing. Anyway, I'm telling them all about the weirdo, and Billy thinks I'm gonna cry 'cos he's upset me! I mean, how stupid is that?

What happened was this.

I was walking Zeus, which is a major thing for me because I really don't like animals. I especially don't like stupid, fat ones that moan at me when I get forced to walk them. It was my turn though and Zeus was in my garden. I took him up and down the street a few times, pulling him along behind me. He moaned and whined all the way too.

I had to dodge a couple of boys who were running full pelt down the street, being chased by an older guy, an ugly bloke who I'd seen around. He had these dirty, matted dreads and two gold teeth and he was always sweating, like drug addicts do. The lads he was after got clean away and he decided to give me a load of grief, which was all I needed on top of having to walk the laziest beast in the world.

He came right up to me and started giving it the large one. 'Yow! You, gal. Wha' yuh a seh?' which I think meant, 'Hi, how are you?'

'Why don't you get lost, you smelly bast—' I shouted at the top of my voice, only I was cut short by Nanny, who appeared out of thin air almost, and stood between me and Mr Butt Ugly.

'Yes, mi bredda? Somethin' I can help the I wid?' Nanny was calm as you like. Polite even.

The bloke looked at Nanny, confused. Then he looked back at me. Funnily enough, he stopped smiling at that point too.

'Wha'?' he said. 'She wit' you, my dread?' He looked at Nanny again.

'Not with me, bwoi. She's my daughter.'

I could see the disbelief in his eyes. He was just standing there on the pavement like a bloated boil on a nasty arse, looking between me and Nanny. Not surprising really. I mean, I couldn't look more different to Nanny if I tried.

'What's up, man?' said Nanny, his tone of voice becoming suddenly harsh. 'I can't have a white daughter? Yuh have two white sisters of yuh own.' He smiled. 'Yah father called Dennis, true?' he said. Mr Ugly couldn't speak. He just nodded lamely, like a toddler being told off. 'Tell yuh father that Nanny said hello.'

I started to giggle at the way the youth had suddenly lost all the air in his chest. He couldn't even look at Nanny by then. All he did was look down at his dirty, baggy jeans, which looked to me like a parachute wrapped around a couple of bamboo shoots.

Nanny spoke up again. 'And, bwoi, get yuh skinny backside out of here before I kick a whole heap a dirty gold toot' down yuh t'roat.'

The guy just skulked off up the road, taking his pea brain and his rancid breath with him.

'Thank you, Nanny,' I said, trying not to cry.

Nanny smiled his big, fat friendly smile. 'It's cool, Ellie,' he said. 'You is a princess but let me tell you – that bwoi deh ain't no prince.'

As Nanny headed off to the shops, I dragged Zeus back towards home, turning into a side street, heading for the entrance to the alley. The ugly bloke had frightened me and I needed to get back nearer home to feel safe now.

The alley runs parallel to our street and it is our Crew's territory, silly as that sounds. We are the only gang who use it.

As we walked along it towards my back gate, we had to dodge dustbins and rubbish bags, cardboard boxes and even an old, rusting pram. A ginger tom cat flashed past us, not even getting a second look out of Zeus but making me jump. The alley has a chain of high walls that run along the back of the gardens on our street, each house linked by a back gate. The walls are charcoal-coloured brick covered in moss and other funny-looking fungal stuff. On the opposite side is the wall of a house which runs about fifty metres down the alley, followed by a tall, dark brown fence which is overhung with even taller trees. Even in the summer the alley is always dark and it gets really gloomy the further down you go. It ends about fifty or a hundred metres on from Billy's back gate. An old brick outhouse blocks the end off, with a door that must have opened onto the alleyway once. I've never seen it open but about three years ago Billy accidentally smashed the glass panel in it with a ball, although he told me that he's never tried to get into it, or the empty house to which it is attached. I've never seen anyone going in or coming out of the place, that's for sure. I wanted to explore the house once, and I did my pouting thing at Della and everyone for about a week when they told me it might be a crack den and was too dangerous. I even tried to play Billy by calling him 'chicken'. Most boys will do anything if you challenge their manhood. But then again, most boys are stupid. Not Billy. He just laughed at me and said, 'Try again, kid,' which led to yet more pouting.

Anyway, as I walked Zeus up to our gate I saw a figure hiding in the shadows at the end of the alley. I could have imagined it, but I know I didn't. It was a tall man, wearing a long black raincoat — the kind of thing businessmen wear over their suits. He had on a hat too, only it didn't match the coat at all. It was a baseball cap. I looked back towards the street, and relaxed a little. It wasn't that far away and I could run quite fast if I really had to. Or I could be in my own back yard within seconds. It was only a metre or two away. I turned and looked for the man again but he had vanished. Or so I thought. I opened the gate to my yard and let Zeus in, before turning to have one last quick look down the alley. The man was now hiding behind a large bin and all I could really see of his face was his eyes. They were this amazing colour – electric blue almost – and he was looking right at me. I shuddered and stifled a scream, noticing a strange, musty smell. It reminded me of rotting rubbish bags mixed with air freshener – you know, the kind that is supposed to smell of roses but ends up making you gag. I'd smelled it before – only last week – so I didn't wait any longer. I turned and slammed the gate shut behind me, locking it, and ran into my house. I was up in my room by the time I took my next breath.

Now I glowered at Billy. 'Why would I just make it up? All the way down to what he was wearing and that nasty smell and everything? And it's the second time I've noticed him. He was there last week as well.'

'Look, Ellie, I'm not saying you are lyin'. I'm not.'

'Yes you are. I mean, I might have been paranoid the first time, yeah. But twice?' I was in full sulk mode.

'Look, you were probably scared and you thought that you . . .'

'Oh, go away, you old man . . .'

I hadn't meant it. But he left anyway. See, men know nothing.

four:

saturday

'Billy, is that your phone bleeping at you?' My mum looked amused. 'Why doesn't it just ring like a normal phone?' She looked up from some work she was doing at the kitchen table.

'It does ring when someone calls, Mum.'

'So that's not someone calling you? What's that noise for then? To tell you that it's hungry?'

I smiled. 'You old fart. That noise tells me I've got a text message.'

My mum made a big show of smelling herself and then the air around her. She grinned and threw her pen at me. She was beautiful, my mum. Long brown hair and a figure that Ellie and Della told me would look wicked on a woman half her age. 'Don't be so rude, Sleepy. Or the next time I see Ellie I'll show her all those lovely baby photos that I've got of you – you know, like the one that I took of you standing naked in the yard wearing only my sunglasses?' She grinned wider.

'Yeah, yeah. You is so funny. For a wrinkly anyways.'

'So, Mr Text Message Man, why haven't you replied to it?'

I looked at my phone. It was Jas. I didn't read the message though. Couldn't be arsed. And anyway I was reading a book about Bob Marley that Nanny had given to me. It was wicked. I looked over at my mum and noticed how tired she was looking. There were frown lines around her eyes and her forehead was all creased. She looked as if she was concentrating on something really complicated. 'What's up, Mum?'

'Usual stuff. Work. More work,' she said through a deep yawn.

'What sort of stuff?'

'Well, you know that I rely on public funding to run the centre and to get paid?'

'Yeah, Babylon money,' I said, joking. Only she wasn't up for a joke.

'It isn't funny, kid. The city council are on this slash and burn cycle where they keep on cutting their spending and they've told us to try and encourage investment from the private sector – businesses and things.'

'Yeah, right. Some chance.'

'Exactly. All those lovely money men who want to see profits coming out of every nook and cranny. Blood from stones . . . that kind of thing.'

'But you don't make . . .'

'Exactly,' she replied, sighing and looking sadder than I had seen her look for a long time. 'Providing refuges for victims of domestic violence is a non-profit service, as is trying to look after all those poor girls who suffer while working the street, drug-counselling and all the other services we need round here.' I'd heard Mum say this kind of thing many times before – it was like a lecture-thing she went off on sometimes – but she carried on regardless.

'Anyway, we all had this meeting earlier with the little Hitlers at the council, and I went mad. Told them we could always start selling booze and drugs to pay for counselling the victims. Only they didn't get the joke.'

'They probably thought it was a good idea.' I tried to smile at her. Thought it might cheer her up.

She just shrugged her shoulders at me. 'Yeah, like firemen starting all the fires before they put them out.'

As she sighed again the kitchen door opened and Della came in with her mum, Sue. Almost before you could blink, the two of them were in the middle of a work debate, one that me and Della had heard different versions of for years. Della gave me a 'let's get out of here before we get roped in' look and yawned dead loud. Right in her mum's direction. Then she got up and walked out of the kitchen, down the hall and out of the front door. I grabbed my phone and followed.

Outside, Della was sitting on the front wall and kicking her feet. She yawned again, then started to play with the braids in her hair.

'I'm so hungry. Your mum making any of that curry?'

'Nah. She's only just got in and Nanny is playing footie on the park.'

'Raas – I'm starvin'!'

It was always a good idea to let Della eat when she was hungry. Otherwise she would get more and more irritable and before you knew it you'd end up nursing a bloody lip just for being there. I moved away from her a little and suggested chips. She nodded and without saying another word headed off up the road to the chippie. I followed again. As I caught her up my phone bleeped at me again. Jas. I was tempted to leave it like I had before but something made me read his message this time. I looked at it and my heart nearly jumped out of my mouth. And then I read it again. And again.

'Dell, forget the chips,' I said, risking a beating but not caring. 'We need to go round Will's and see him and Jas.'

'But I'm—'

'Dell, trust me. It's important,' I replied, turning in the opposite direction and heading off to Will's house, a few streets from mine.

Della waited a moment and then spun round and followed me. She was mumbling under her breath about wanting to 'lick' me in the back of the head with her fist. Man, she was one dangerous sister when she was hungry. I had a feeling she was going to forget all about her chips once we got to Will's house though. Missing one bag of chips wouldn't be important once she'd heard what Will and Jas had to say. Believe me.

Will showed us up to his room in complete silence, his finger to his lips. No 'hello' or 'how are you?' Not even the offer of a glass of council pop, which was what Will liked to call tap water. We walked into his room, shutting the door behind us, then locking it from the inside. Jas was sitting on Will's bed, waiting for us. Della sat down next to him and I stood in the narrow gap that ran between the bed and a self-built shelving unit that was fixed to the wall. It held Will's turntable, mixer, stereo and fast-growing selection of tunes. The room was covered in floral wallpaper, nasty green flowers on an even nastier light beige background. In turn, the eyeball-damaging excuse for wall decoration was almost completely covered in posters and photos and flyers promoting club nights that Will had never been to, as well as one or two that he had.

Will stayed at the foot of his bed and between him and Jas sat a black canvas bag with a zip across the top of it. Della was looking at Jas and then Will and back again, asking with her fiery eyes and her flared nostrils for them to explain exactly why they had dragged her away from her chips. No one said a word. From Jas's message, I knew what was in the bag and my heart really felt like it was in my mouth.

'Well?' asked Della. 'Is one of you tossers gonna tell me why I'm still hungry or is this one of those boy things?'

I looked at Will, who looked at Jas, and then Jas returned the ball to my court.

'Not me, dread,' I said. 'I didn't find it.'

'Find what, you gimps?' Della glared at me.

I tried not to smile and pointed at Jas, who mouthed the words, 'Thanks, you wanker,' and then picked up the bag. 'It's in there,' he offered, pointing at the bag and looking at Della.

She just blinked at him. You could almost see the sarcasm about to explode out of her head. 'What is in de bag, lickle bwoi? Me dinner?' She kissed her teeth.

'No, there's—' he began, only to be cut off by me.

'We should call Ellie – this is a Crew thing. She should be here.'

Jas shut up, let go a big smile and winked at Della, who just kissed her teeth at him too.

'You boys carry on playin' with yourselves – is what you ah do best anyways – I'll go round and get Ellie. This

31

. . . this . . . sweaty lickle room could use a bit of feminine balance anyway.'

Will just grinned back at her before picking up a piece of pool chalk from a shelf behind him and throwing it at her head. Della moved out of the line of fire and the blue square bounced off Jas's head, leaving a smudge. Everyone started laughing and suddenly Della made a grab for the bag.

'Before I go waste my lickle sister's time, lemme see what you got in deh,' she said.

Instantly me, Jas and Will tried to stop her. She was pulling the bag one way and we were all trying to pull it another.

'What . . . you got . . . in here?' she said between tugs. 'Best not be no dutty nasty . . .'

'It's not porn,' I said as I tried to separate Jas and Della.

'Oh, for . . .' I could tell she was about to explode.

'It's . . .'

As I spoke the contents of the bag cascaded out and landed on Will's bed, on the floor, everywhere. Della's jaw dropped.

'. . . money.'

Ellie looked at me in disbelief. I reckon she was sitting there thinking about how many pairs of trainers she could get with all the money that Jas and Will had found. 'How much is there?' she asked as Della finished counting it all.

'About fifteen grand, man,' replied Della, dropping the money back into the bag.

'Bwoi, I could get a whole heap of trainers with fifteen

big ones, man.'

I got up from Will's bed and shook my head. 'And a whole heap of grief too – from whoever this dough belongs to.'

'No one seen us find the bag, man.' Jas was eyeing it as he spoke. 'Thing was hidden behind a bin in our alley. Way I see things, Billy, that money is ours, man. Tax free an' not a cent of VAT.'

'How do you know that no one saw you?' I asked.

''Cos there weren't no other man in the alley. Jus' me an' Willy over there. It was early, man. No one else was around that early this morning.'

'Hey, bhangra queen – me name ain't Willy.'

'Come along now, boys,' said Ellie, smiling. 'Let's not be catty – it's so Graham Norton, don't you think?'

Will and Jas told her to shut up in unison. Ellie just laughed. One–nil to the blonde girl.

Della didn't join in with Ellie's fun, eyeing us all instead. I knew what she was thinking. It was exactly what I was thinking too. Sure, all that money was tempting. I had already had a daydream about starring in my own hip-hop lifestyle video. But then reality had slipped in uninvited, and three letters lit up in front of my eyes in a big, bright neon glow: N-A-H. I was wondering if Della could see the same images that were playing themselves out in my mind when she spoke up.

'Right, let's all forget the dreams about buyin' new clothes and shit that I know we all been having and think about this like intelligent people and not greedy lickle Babylon.'

Will and Jas groaned together, as Della continued. 'See, that money,' she said, pointing at the bag, 'ain't just fallen out the sky. Somebody left it there, hidden in the alley, most probably for a good reason.'

'Is what good reason could a man have to leave fifteen grand in an alleyway, man?' Will kissed his teeth as he finished.

'Hush yuh mout', William, an' listen. If it weren't left for a reason then it was a mistake. Either way . . .' Della held up the bag for us all to see. As if we weren't looking at it anyway. 'This money in this bag is dirty money. Come on, guys, it's obvious. It's got to be connected to a drug gang or to a robbery or even one of them slave-traders.'

When she said slave-trader, Della meant pimp, but she had never used that word. Not in all the time I had known her. Even hearing it on other people's lips made her flinch and her eyes well up with angry tears.

'So if we keep the money – then whoever it belongs to is gonna come looking for us. We're the only gang that use that alley. It's our alley. No one else goes in there if they can help it. Man, *Zeus* thinks it's dirty an' he's a *dog*.'

'Dell, ain't no one gonna find out 'cos no one seen us take the bag,' countered Jas.

'Is how yuh know that?' replied Della, but in a notice-ably lighter tone of voice to Jas than to Will. Thing was, I'd already denied her food and I wasn't about to push my luck by pointing out her soft spot for my mate.

'So what are we going to do?' added Ellie. 'And can we decide soon because I'm hungry.'

'Yeah, so am I,' agreed Della, 'and I'm about ready fe kill a bwoi an' eat him.'

I took the lead and the bag from Della. Looking round

at the rest of the crew, I waited a few moments and then handed the bag back to Will. 'We ain't doing nothing with it tonight. We'll take a vote on it and whatever we decide to do with it, for tonight at least, we'll leave it with Will. Agreed?'

Everyone nodded.

'So all in favour of keeping the money?'

Jas and Will looked at each other and then nodded.

'Puttin' it back ... ?'

'Nah,' said Della. 'It's our alley. If we put it back, someone else could nick it and we'd still get all the shit.'

'OK, then, handin' it in . . . ?'

Ellie and Della nodded without any hesitation.

'Looks like you got the casting vote, my dan,' laughed Jas. 'As always.'

'I dunno,' I said. I really wasn't that sure what we should do.

'Well then, what's the point of—?' began Della and Jas together.

'Let's leave it for a few days,' I said. 'That way we can think about it properly. Everyone up for that?'

Slowly they all nodded.

'Cool. Now we can go get some food.' I looked at Della.

'About time too,' she said.

We all left Will's house together and headed for the chippie. Jas and Della went on ahead. Jas whispered something in her ear and she giggled, prompting Will to give me a look that said, 'What's going on there then?'

I shrugged as Ellie just did her usual mocking and moaning routine. '. . . but Will, I don't want chips. I want pizza. Can I have pizza . . . please, Dad,' she said, smiling.

Will raised his eyebrows. 'Man, Ellie, I've told you before. Don't keep calling me Dad. It's sick.'

'Oh, please let me have pizza. *Please*. I'll stop calling you Dad, old man . . . *please*.'

five:

monday afternoon

I was walking back from town a couple of days later, getting soaked in a thunderstorm. Rainwater dripped from my face and hair and ran down my back, ice-cold needles of it that made me shiver. It was yet another typical English summer. Despite the rain, I still had the money on my mind. I had the casting vote and I didn't want it. Whatever I decided, either way, I was going to upset someone. Part of me wanted to keep it. Big time. But the more I thought about it, the more I was convinced that we had to get rid of it – hand it in. I had decided to ask Nanny for his advice and was on my way home to see him.

The walk from town took me past the back of the train station, an old Victorian building that had recently been put through a clean-up. It was a local hangout for all the junkies and sex-workers, male and female, as well as a gateway to the rest of the country. I walked through its car park, past turbaned taxi-drivers and their customers. A high-speed train was pulling in as I jumped the car-park fence onto the iron road bridge that linked the town centre to the ghetto. The bridge was black with grime and I wondered if anyone would ever clean it up like they had the station. It wasn't very likely. After all, the train station was the first thing that visitors to the city would see. My area was the last thing the council wanted anyone new in town to see.

I walked on through the estate, letting my mind stray wherever it pleased. It was what I did. Think. Mostly too much. My mum told me once that I was born with a furrowed brow. She told me I even frowned in my sleep. I believed her too.

The money continued to bother my thoughts as I passed a line of cars parked up at the kerbside, people leaning in and drivers and passengers passing things out. Money, drugs, even a CD player. Twice, I saw police cars pass by and each time the occupants gave me the once-over, the drowned ghetto rat making his way home over dirty, rubbish-strewn streets. Pure suspicion passed across their faces, just like it always did. I walked into the community centre car park, cutting a corner. My mum was based in the centre and I wondered if she was about. Normally I'd stop to say hello but the rain was still battering down so I carried on, wanting to get home.

When I got there, Nanny was in the kitchen making some soup and listening to Black Uhuru, this old reggae band. I got a towel and dried my head with it as Nanny tried to sing along to one of the songs.

'Man, that voice isn't what it could be, is it?' I said, grinning as I let my earlier thoughts disappear into the void at the back of my brain, my own personal recycle bin – a bin that never got emptied.

'Wha'? And yours is, man?' Nanny threw a slice of pepper at me and then carried on singing.

'What's the song called then?' I asked, opening the fridge to get myself some juice.

'"What Is Life", man.'

'I dunno. You tell me, dread,' I said, pleased with my little joke.

'Life is just a test, y'know. Just some man Jah a bless.' Nanny ignored my attempt at humour.

I decided to ask him straight out about the money. 'Talking of tests – I've got a problem, Nanny. I need your help with something.'

'Man, I hope you haven't got into trouble with the police again, Sleepy.'

'Nah, man, nothing that serious.'

'A good ting too, my yout'. Not even I would be able to stop yuh muddah from kill you this time.'

I looked away, remembering my brush with the police over the joyriding. I let it go. 'I have more of a moral dilemma, Nanny.'

He smiled. 'Moral dilemma is easy, man. Yuh have right and yuh have wrong and in da middle yuh have everyting else. The real world.'

'What you on about, man?'

'Well, is like this. What you think is wrong another man might think is right. People have different ways of looking at the world. Could be 'cos of dem religion or the politics they believe in. Could be down to any number of t'ings.'

'Like how I don't agree with racists, you mean.'

Nanny smiled again. 'Yeah, man. Is one example. Now, why don't yuh explain what yuh problem is.'

'Money. It's a problem with money, Nan.'

Nanny took a wooden spoon and stirred his soup, not

answering me for a while. 'Money is a problem for ninety per cent of the world, Sleepy,' he replied thoughtfully.

'Don't call me that, Nan. It makes me feel like I'm five years old again.'

'So, tell me.' The wooden spoon he was holding and pointing in my direction let loose flecks of soup that splashed the table in front of me. I wiped a drop away with a finger.

'Jas and Will found some money a few days ago. In the alley. In a bag.'

Nanny frowned, returning his wooden spoon to the pot. 'How much money, Billy?' he asked before stirring the soup again.

'A lot of money. In crumpled notes.'

'An' yuh nah know what to do wid it, yes?' I knew that Nanny would know exactly what my dilemma would be. All he needed were the facts.

'Yeah. The lads wanna keep it but Dell and Ellie wanna hand it in to the police.'

'An' because you run de Crew like democracy you get the final vote.'

'Yeah,' I said. 'Somethin' like that.'

'Let me finish making this soup and I'll come talk to you,' he said, frowning some more.

I went up to my bedroom and waited for him. It wasn't that Nanny had to have some huge debate with himself about my dilemma. He already had an answer. He just wanted me to go away and think about it for myself. Properly. He always did that. Once, a few years earlier, I got into trouble over a broken window and I had lied through my teeth to cover myself. Only Nanny knew straight away. He saw straight through my lie and let me know. And then he let me come to my own conclusion about what I had to do to make up for it. Nanny, the dreadlocked psychologist. Like *Cracker* on weed.

six:

monday, 9 p.m.

'We just saw that bloke in the alley, Billy. The one Baby was on about.'

Jas was excited and out of breath, talking nineteen to the dozen as Will nodded in agreement. I had been sitting around, mooching, waiting for Nanny to get back to me, only he had gone out somewhere and forgotten about me. Or so I thought. Around nine that night Jas and Will had come round, breathless and sweaty.

'How do you know it was the same man?' I asked them. It could have been anyone.

'Well . . . I suppose we don't really,' offered Will haltingly. 'But he looked just like she said and he legged it when we turned up and had a go at him.'

'So you two clowns just chased some innocent man out of the alley and halfway round the ghetto without knowing for sure that he had done anything?'

'Er . . . yeah,' replied Jas, grinning. 'How cool is that, man. Playin' like feds, man. Five-O.'

'Feds is what you're gonna have on your ass when that bloke reports you to the police. And what if that was *his* money we've got. He could have come back for it!'

'Nah,' replied Jas, dismissive. 'He weren't the kind of man to have any serious money wid him. The man's just a nonce, Billy. He was hassling Ellie. Man, we couldn't let that go.'

Mr Kick-boxer gave me a self-righteous look before grinning again but Will suddenly began to look worried. He scratched his head. 'Boy, could be he was just some other bloke, y'know. Not the same one that Ellie saw.'

'Could be,' I began, trying not to laugh, 'that you two are gonna be calling my ass from the police station, talking about bail.'

First Will started to laugh, then me, and finally Jas. I could just imagine Jas and Will on the phone from the cells, begging me to get them out. Little boys playing at big men.

'Forget it anyway,' said Will. 'Mofo was that scared he ain't gonna leave his house for a week.'

We all started laughing again. At the time it was funny. Will and Jas chasing some random man from the alley for no good reason and no proof that he had done anything wrong. Man, you wouldn't believe how wrong we all were.

Nanny turned up at around ten with a big bag of weed and a smile on his face. The lads had gone and my mum was at the kitchen table, on the phone to a friend. Nanny waited for my mum to get off the phone and then gave her a kiss. She looked at the bag of weed and shook her head, smiling.

'What happened to you earlier?' I asked him, putting down my magazine.

'I had to go out, Billy. Things to do.'

'What, like buying herb?' I pointed at the bag.

'And checking out a little something for you and your friends.'

As he spoke my mum gave me a strange look. It was her 'mother's intuition' and it was scary. She could sense trouble from a mile away, especially if it involved me. 'What little something are you on about?' she asked, frowning.

Nanny held up his hands and shrugged, as if to say, 'Don't ask me to explain.'

'Well, Billy, what have you lot done this time?' My mum gave me her look. If you could call a glare gentle, then that's what it was. Gentle – yet deadly.

'We ain't done anything,' I told her, which was basically true if you didn't count Jas and Will scaring the life out of some poor bloke.

'We *haven't* done anything, Billy. You can save your bad boy language for your mates.'

'Well we haven't. We just *found* something, that's all.'

My mum sighed. 'Just like you found that condom in your jeans that time? Or the ecstasy tablets that just *appeared* in that jacket pocket last year?'

'That's not fair, Mum. You know that wasn't my jacket and I'd tell you if I was thinking of doing Es or any other drug. I don't feel that I have to hide things from you . . .'

'But you do anyway?' She wore this questioning look. One that I had to avoid.

Luckily Nanny jumped in to rescue me. Sort of. 'Hol' on, darlin'. They never do a ting wrong. They jus' find a lickle money in the alley out back.'

I groaned.

'Exactly *how much* money are we talking about?'

44

I hesitated and looked away. Anywhere but at my mum. 'Er . . . quite a lot, Mum,' I said, immediately realizing that I was about to get a rocket.

'Don't play me, young man. I'm not an idiot. How much?' Man, she was getting angry.

'Fifteen . . .'

'Fifteen pounds?'

'Grand.'

I let the word fall out of my mouth rather than making any attempt to project it, hoping that my mum wouldn't hear what I had said, and then looked at Nanny, who just whistled at the amount.

'Fifteen thousand pounds? *Fifteen?* . . . What the hell were you doing . . . ?' she began.

'Jas and Will found it. Someone left a holdall in the alley and the lads went to check it out. They found the money inside it.' I felt like a kid again. Scared of what my mum's reaction was going to be.

She sat and thought for a minute. I tried to carry on talking but she just held her hand in my face to tell me to shut up. Nanny started to build himself a spliff but he got told to stop too. And he did. Without even a murmur of complaint. Mum looked at Nanny and then at me. 'And I suppose you can't decide whether or not to keep the money or hand it in to the police? Or maybe just put the bag *back*?' Another gentle glare.

'Yeah,' I replied. 'That's it exactly.'

She just shook her head. 'Now let me see. Who normally carries fifteen grand around in black bags and then leaves it in an alley – in the middle of an area where drug dealing and sex-work are just two of the many dubious activities that go on?' There was real, heavy sarcasm in her voice. 'Let's see now . . . who could that be?' She looked from me to Nanny and back again.

'Look, Mum, I know—' I began, regretting it.

'You don't know anything, Billy. Otherwise you wouldn't even be thinking about it. You should have put the sodding bag back where you found it or handed it in to the police. That would make it their problem. Now it's yours.'

'I know . . .' I began again.

'What do you *know*? That it belongs to a drug dealer or a *pimp*? That whoever left it there left it to be *picked up*? That the people it belongs to are already *out there* looking for it?'

'Yeah.' I replied quietly, beginning to feel stupid. My mum had a way of doing that to me when I was messing things up.

'You aren't stupid, Billy. None of you are. But you don't half do some stupid things.' It was like she could read my mind.

'I don't think we can put it back. It will have been missed by now. We'll have to hand it in, Mum. Tomorrow.' There was that little kid feeling again.

'No, no you won't. You'll take Nanny with you and go and hand it in right now. Tonight.'

Nanny looked shocked. He didn't like seeing the police on the streets, never mind going to the station. It would probably make the skin at the back of his neck crawl. His frown followed mine, only his was deeper. 'Why mek me take dem to the station? Me nuh deal wid police, man.'

'Because I'm tired and I've spent all day arguing with one of their neighbourhood liaison officers. If I see another policeman tonight I think I might just lose it.'

Nanny smiled but still looked kind of unsure about going to the station. In the end, seeing that my mum wasn't going to budge, he resigned himself to it. 'Yuh muddah is right, Billy. Is Babylon money so we must tek it back to dem.'

'It's drug money,' I said. 'It don't belong to the police.'

'Police. Criminal. Is the same shit to me.'

'What if they saw the lads take it, Billy? The people who it belongs to?' added my mum. She was looking concerned now.

'They didn't,' I replied, trying to sound like I wasn't concerned myself.

'Billy, don't be so naive. Anyone who knows this area knows that you and your mates use that alley like it belongs to you alone. They'll know it's one of you that took it. The kind of people who have fifteen thousand pounds in black bags don't mess about. Trust me, kid. I know.'

I couldn't argue with her. She *did* know. She knew all about life on the streets and she knew all about the bad men that operated in the area. I could see in her eyes that she was back on the streets now, back in her past. She still found it hard to deal with. Her face darkened and she touched her left cheekbone. A punter had beaten her up once, smashing the bone, and whenever anyone mentioned the past or anything linked with it, she instantly touched it, as if by reflex. I thought I would start crying. I wanted to. I hated that my mum had all this shit in her past that I could never help her to get over. It cut me up.

'Rita, chill,' said Nanny. 'We can tek it to the police. That way it's out of we hands. It gonna be more danger- ous still if we put de ting back now.'

My mum didn't look totally convinced. She looked at me with suspicion.

'Now?' she said, a question in her voice. 'How long have you *had* this money then, Billy?'

'Er . . . three days,' I admitted. 'Jas and Will found it Saturday morning.'

'Well, no argument then,' Mum said firmly. 'They'll have missed it by now for sure, so you'd better get your Crew together and get your sorry arses down the station. *Now!*'

She was right. I rang Jas and told him what was going to happen. He had just had the same conversation with his own mother. He told me that he realized that they were right, his mum and mine. There was way too much grief involved – keeping hold of the money or putting it back just wasn't an option any longer. I told him to go and get Will and bring the money with them but then decided it was probably safer for Nanny and me to go over to them. My mum was right. We had no idea if anyone was watching or not. And if someone was watching and saw two youths walking down the road with their bag . . . Well, you can figure out the rest.

seven:

monday, 11 p.m.

The walk to the police station took us back over the iron bridge and across the dual carriageway where I had first met Ellie. On the way, Nanny was talking to Jas about his kick boxing and Will was complaining about how he was going to have a problem getting back into his house. He had sneaked out of his bedroom window and over a low roof to get out. His old man would have gone spare if he had come out at such a late hour. Sometimes he treated Will like he was still a child – which really wound Will up. After all, he was sixteen now *and* working.

The police station was a huge grey box – a complete eyesore in an already architecturally impaired area. There was a new annexe to the back of the station where the public entrance was. I had never been in that way. The last time I had visited, it had been through the huge security gates around the back and I had been chauffeured there by my local neighbourhood storm trooper. Even Nanny looked worried about visiting what he usually called 'Babylon Regional Office'.

'Hey, Nanny – what's up? You look scared, man!' I asked, smiling.

'I ain't scared, Billy – I just don't like coming here. Is like the hairs on me neck stand on end an' I wan' run away ev'ry time me on yah.'

I think he was saying that the police made him nervous but you never can tell with Nanny.

'Them bring me 'ere back in the riots, man. I was tryin' to stop de yout' from mash up the high street an' get dem to organize. I never even fling one stone 'pon de beast but they still lock I up in prison for one year. Jus' on the word a one policeman.'

'Which riots, man?' asked Will.

'Man, back in the ghetto Summer of Love, youthman. Nineteen eighty-one. None a yuh even born yet. Man, de whole a England get mash up.'

'What? Like what the youths in the north been doin' last year?'

'Yeah, man, all due to Babylon treating we as subhuman.'

'Boy, it's coming like nothing ever changes, man,' I said, shaking my head.

Jas decided to make a contribution to the conversation. 'So, like you was in prison? Man, that's cool, Nanny. You is one bad bwoi.'

Nanny gave Jas a pitiful look and shook his head. 'There is nothing good or cool about prison, Jas. Prison is an ugly place. It break a man's spirit. Jah meant fe a man to fly free like a bird, not sit in a cell like so many bull ina pen.'

The reception area of the station was a cold blue and grey colour. Nanny walked up to the desk and sat the bag on the counter. The copper behind the desk looked down his long nose at Nanny and then at the bag. He gave me, Will and Jas the same treatment.

'Can I help you?' he asked, not looking at any of us.

'Yes, man. We would like to hand in this bag a' money dat de man deh,' Nanny began, pointing at us, '. . . dat dem man find in de alley. Sah.'

I wanted to laugh. Nanny was deliberately talking in a way that the policeman would find hard to understand. And calling him 'sir' after the sentence was as sarcastic as a weed-smoking, Jah-loving man like Nanny could get.

'I see,' said the policeman. He looked us over again. 'And what country do we all come from then?' he said, smiling.

'You're funny, man.' Will looked immediately angry. 'We're English.'

'And what about your . . .' he began, giving Nanny the kind of look that most people save for something stuck to the sole of their shoe . . . 'your mate here. The one who can't speak English.'

'Actually I can speak the Queen's tongue rather well,' said Nanny, causing even my jaw to drop. *How* posh was his voice?

'So you do speak—' began the copper.

'Nah, man. Least not wid Babylon.'

The policeman turned his attention to the bag. He picked it up and studied it. 'It's quite heavy,' he said, putting it down and trying to smile, something he didn't quite manage.

'Yeah, well, it's full,' I said.

'With what? It's not got a bomb in it, has it? Can't be too careful these days . . .' He sneered at us.

51

'Yuh tek de piss nuh, man?' said Nanny in a serious tone of voice.

'If you like, sir,' the policeman answered but in a tone that said he didn't really give a shit.

'Do you have a superior officer, little Babylon? Yuh know – like yuh master?' Nanny turned and winked at me.

'You don't need to see anyone other than me. It's only a few pounds and a stolen bag.'

'The bag ain't stolen and if you think fifteen grand is a few pounds then you must be on the take, man,' added Will.

The copper looked shocked all of a sudden. He opened the bag and looked at the contents. My holiday money. Ellie's new trainers. Will's new decks and mixer. He picked up the phone on his desk and called someone else down. '. . . three teens and a gentleman . . . yeah the bloke's IC3.' He put the receiver down and turned to us. 'DI Ratnett is on his way down,' he said before turning away.

Nanny grinned at the man's name.

We were all interviewed about the money separately. When it came to my turn, I spent five minutes explaining to DI Ratnett that the money might well be stolen but that I hadn't stolen it and nor had anyone else in the Crew. He then spent the next twenty minutes asking me if I knew whether Jas or Will needed money. Whether they had drug habits. If they indulged in any criminal activity like dealing crack. As he asked his questions I tried not to breathe in the stale air around him. It smelt of cigarettes and coffee and he carried a faint whiff of cleanliness masked by overpowering body odour. I didn't even want to think about when he had last showered. It felt as though we were being treated as the criminals when all we had done was find the money and hand it in. Fair enough, we had told a prearranged little white lie about when we had found the money, claiming that it had been earlier that evening.

'Are you sure it was this evening?' he kept on asking me.

'Yeah, I'm sure.'

'You didn't keep it for few days? Think about whether or not to keep it? Take a little bonus for yourself? I know it would be tempting.'

'No,' I said, getting more and more pissed off.

'After all, we're all human,' he said, smiling in a way that suggested someone had held a gun to his head and made him do it.

All human? Not you, I thought to myself. Dutty Babylon.

'And you've no idea who it might belong to, this money?'

'Like I keep telling you, no.' Man, he was winding me up.

'Local dealer, maybe? Pimp?'

'Man, I told you. I ain't got no clue where it came from and I don't care – you gets me? Why you tryin' to make me and my Crew out to be criminals?'

'Well, you are, aren't you? I've seen a copy of your arrest sheet. Juvenile delinquent, I believe you would have been called in the old, non-politically correct days.'

'That's got sweet f.a. to do with this,' I said. 'Besides, I never got done for stealing no money.'

'Money . . . cars – what's the difference, Billy?'

'You don't know me so don't call me Billy. I ain't done anything so just finish your stupid questions and let me go.'

'Stupid would be you trying to tell me what to do, son. I don't take kindly to people like you ordering me about.'

'*People like me?* What the——?' I began angrily.

'Watch it, son!' I calmed down before he continued. 'And remember – I've got my eye on you.'

'Where'd you get your lines, man? Off *The Bill*?' I said as I walked out of the interview room.

Man, I hated people like Ratnett.

On the way home I found out that we had all been treated in the same way, with Nanny getting the worst of it. They had asked him what he was doing with us. Whether he was Will's father. When he told them that he was my step-dad, kind of, they had asked him if he had any previous convictions. Whether he liked young boys. Really nasty stuff. I was fuming. I wanted to tell my mum when we got in and I told him so.

'Leave it, Billy. Your mum got enough on her plate without having to worry about the dutty mind of some Babylonian. Forget them, man. We nuh deal wid dem.'

We walked through the same streets that I had walked earlier, losing Jas and a very pissed off and angry Will at the end of our street. I told them that I'd call them in the morning and walked on with Nanny. Halfway down our street there was a police car sitting at the kerb with its lights flashing. I looked at Nanny, who nodded, reading my thoughts. The car was outside our house! I took off at a sprint, Nanny right behind, and as I reached my house I saw that the downstairs front window had been smashed. My mum was standing outside, talking to a female copper.

'Mum! What happened? Are you all right?' I pushed past the copper and hugged her.

'It's OK, Billy,' she replied. 'Someone threw a brick through the window, that's all.'

'What do you mean, that's all? Did you see who did it?' I was well angry.

'No. Whoever it was ran off before I got a chance. It's just some nasty little racist. There's been a few attacks this week on the mosque and the community centre, because of the local elections. We'll board it up and sort it out later. Come on, make your mum a cup of tea, Sleepy.'

'Man, sometimes I hate this country. They dis us for not being patriotic and then they treat us like animals.'

My mum gave me a strange look. It said, 'Don't overreact.'

'It's not just this,' I said, feeling a little silly because the policewoman was looking at me like I was a basket case. 'I'll tell you inside.' The policewoman continued to stare at me. 'What you looking at? Can't you go and arrest some crack dealers or something?'

eight:

Wednesday, 6 p.m.

*O*n *the evening it happened I was out walking the mutt
again. He was pulling me this way and that way and I was
having a hard time holding onto him. Stupid dog. I had tried my
usual trick with Billy — you know, pouting, begging, anything to
get him to take the bloody thing for a walk. And do you know
what he did? He laughed at me. He's such a man. A boy. I mean,
I was trying to get him to cover my responsibilities but still . . .*

*It was cold and wet, which was typical, and I wasn't wearing
a coat, which was even more typical. Of me. We walked past a
gang of lads who were hanging around by a couple of phone boxes
and an off-licence. They seemed to be taking turns to go in and
try to hoodwink the owner into selling them booze. As we got
about a hundred metres away from them I heard a police-car siren
and turned to see the lads running in all directions as the car
pulled up. One of them was holding what looked like a four-pack
of beers as he ran. The policemen took off after him. I shook my
head. It was just a typical summer night. Full of silly little boys
committing silly little crimes. I turned again and carried on
dragging Zeus up the road. He was whimpering at me, as if I
would take pity on him and turn back, but I wasn't playing his
game — just like Billy hadn't played mine. Not that I was*

comparing Billy to a dog. No, Billy was just a miserable old man.

The first time I realized something was wrong was when I turned down a side street with Zeus and made for home. I didn't notice the green car at first – on the main road there was loads of traffic and anyway, why would I have been looking at cars? But on the side street it was the only car that passed me. Three times.

I pulled Zeus on a little further and then took a left down another street, which ran parallel to the main road up to the park. I was halfway down the road when the green car passed me for a fourth time. This time it slowed right down and I was about to swear at the occupants at the top of my voice when Zeus made this deep growling sound and bolted from my grip. He turned sideways and then jumped at something behind me. I heard a horrible cry of pain and turned to see Zeus with his teeth stuck into the arm of a tall man in a long, dark coat.

I tried to scream but it came out with no volume and I was frozen, stuck to the same spot. The man punched and kicked at Zeus, trying to get him to let go of his arm. I screamed again and still made no sound and then I kicked the man between his legs. I mean, he was kicking Zeus. Suddenly Zeus let go, whimpered and ran off. Ran off! Leaving me with an irate pervert in a long coat, blood dripping from a bite wound in his arm and with a sharp pain in his groin that I had inflicted. I had just one thought going through my mind – well, two actually. The first was that I was dead and the second was 'bloody dog'.

I turned and ran, the volume of my screams reaching full capacity. I sprinted straight ahead towards the safety of the main road, hoping to get to it and lose the pervert in the coat. But the ground underfoot was slippery with the rain and I lost my footing, went over on my ankle and hit my head against the side of a parked car. I was crying by then – really scared but at the same time really angry. Angry with the dog for running off and angry with the man. My head was spinning as I tried to get up and all I wanted was to be rescued by my dad or by Billy like the first time we met. Or Nanny. Anyone. And where were the police when you needed—?

The man grabbed me from behind, his forearm around my throat. I tried to scream. To bite him. I kicked out and struggled and wriggled and fought but it was no use. His arm was so tight around my throat that I was gagging and I could feel myself beginning to pass out. I could smell his aftershave, which seemed to have a strange musky edge to it, and I noticed his fingernails, which were long like a woman's and dirty beyond belief. You see, I was trying to see as much of my attacker as possible so that I'd be able to tell the police afterwards. It was something that a girl on a TV documentary had said she had done. Isn't it funny what goes through your mind sometimes? I think that I struggled right up until I passed out — I don't know for sure, but the last thing that I remember thinking was, Please don't kill me, please don't kill me. I don't want to die. I want my mum. I WANT MY MUM! . . .

nine:

wednesday, 8 p.m.

'I was wondering if you had seen Ellie today?'
I was sitting at the kitchen table reading the newspaper when Ellie's dad came in with my mum. Looking up at Mr Sykes, I shook my head. No. At least not since she had taken Zeus out.

'It's just that she hasn't come in yet and she's not answering her phone. She never misses her tea,' he said, sounding worried.

Like an idiot I ignored the tension in his voice. 'Yeah, I know. For such a fit girl she loves her food, don't she?'

I hadn't meant fit as in *fit* – just fit as in healthy, but Mr Sykes raised an eyebrow at me through his worried expression. I felt about Kylie Minogue big.

'Billy, why don't I make Ellie's dad a cup of tea and let you ring round your friends. See if anyone has seen her.' My mum glared at me.

I got up, chucking my paper on the table, trying to avoid Mr Sykes' gaze. Man, sometimes I can be a right knobhead. 'I'll try Della first. She usually ends up round there,' I said, trying to sound reassuring and failing badly.

I was beginning to get worried myself. I mean, Ellie

was usually very good about not being late back from anywhere. She always rang one of the Crew or her mum. Man, she rang her mum five times a day anyway. Even when she was at mine – and I lived next door.

I began to get scared when Della told me that Ellie had been planning to get me to take her to the cinema. I hadn't heard from her since she had taken Zeus for that walk. Zeus was missing too and I thought about mentioning it but then I thought again. No point worrying her and Mr Sykes any further, especially as Ellie would probably walk in the door any second. Or so I thought. I rang Jas and Will, asking if they had seen Ellie. They hadn't. I told them to come round, explaining that as we couldn't find her, we should go out and look for her. Della and Sue turned up just as I put my phone away, Sue joining my mum and Mr Sykes in the kitchen while Della and I went up to my room.

'Any of the others seen her, Billy?' Della looked worried.

'No, Dell.'

'Billy, you best call Beavis and Butthead. We need to go look for my sister.' Her eyes were beginning to water.

'Already done it, Della. Look, she'll be all right. She's probably sulking somewhere because I made her take Zeus out.' I was beginning to wish I had given in and taken the dog out myself.

'Out in this weather? Billy, have you even seen how much it's rainin' out deh?'

'Yeah.' The feeling began to grow. It was my fault.

'I'm soaked up to my tits just from gettin' out my mum's car.'

'Well, maybe she's at a friend's house. You know –

someone from school and that.' It was a possibility, but I didn't believe it. She *would* have phoned someone. 'We'd better go look for her,' I said, desperate to do something.

'Yeah. When the other two decide to show up.'

'No. You and me can go out now. I'll call Jas and tell him to go looking with Will. We can cover more ground if we split up.'

'You know what? That's the best idea you've had tonight.' She looked at me with her watery eyes.

'Are you angry, Dell?'

'No, I ain't angry. I'm just scared.'

I put my arm round her and pulled her closer to me. 'Hey, kid. It's OK. Don't get too worried. We don't know that anything's wrong yet.'

'Yeah we do, Billy. We do. Ellie wouldn't just stay out. She's too sensible for that. And you know it's true.'

I tried to stop Della from crying but I couldn't and deep down, in the pit of my stomach, I was scared too. Every day on the news there were different stories about abductions and murder and that. Not to Ellie. Not our Ellie. Everyone knew Ellie round here. No one would harm her – would they? She was like our little baby sister. I started to get really angry inside.

Ellie's mum came over to the house around ten that evening. She had been waiting at home just in case Ellie rang. She hadn't. Mr Sykes sat staring at the television – I had switched it on to break the silence that had descended over the kitchen. Sue, Della's mum, was helping to make everyone some food and tea, talking in a whisper to my mum.

Della and I had been out looking for Ellie around the

local streets, along with Jas and Will. Between us we had split the ghetto in two and covered it that way. We had asked all the other crews, the working girls who were just coming out on the streets, the dealers, pimps, winos. Everyone. Della had even gone straight up to the head of an older crew, that nutter Busta. Busta didn't like me and he'd laughed at us, which made Della angrier than usual. Man, even I hadn't spotted the punch that she let loose to the side of that boy's head. It was a major problem now, though – one that I was going to have to sort out. It was the stupid way that things round our area worked. We had to run off before he had a chance to call his boys, but I was going to have to face them all tomorrow or the next day. Soon.

'I never meant to punch the bwoi, Billy,' Della told me.

We were both wet and cold and drinking tea. Jas and Will had just turned up with no news and I had told them about the trouble with Busta.

'What does it matter, man?' Jas had his face set in its baddest mask. Nanny called it a 'screwface'.

'Yeah, who cares?' agreed Will. 'The babygirl is missing and all we can do is beat up next man.'

Bad move.

'Say what? You havin' a go at me, bad bwoi?' shouted Della, her eyes almost glowing.

'Relax, Della. I ain't having a go at you. Busta can wait. I ain't bothered by him.'

'Yeah, that bwoi will get his beating soon enough. Right now we got to find Ellie,' added Jas.

Della's glare softened as she looked at Jas and she pulled her chair closer to him.

'Billy, can you come over here, please?' It was my

62

mum. She and Sue were standing by the kitchen sink with Ellie's mum, Marge.

I got up and went over, rivulets of water running out of my hair and down my neck, making me shiver. 'What's up, Mum?' I asked, smiling at Mrs Sykes, hoping that it would stop her from worrying too much. Fat chance.

'Let's get this straight. None of you found out anything?'

'No,' I told her. 'No one's seen her anywhere.'

'And the dog is still missing?' added Sue.

'Yeah. I don't know where they could be.'

'That's it then,' started Ellie's mum. 'We need to call the police. Report her missing.'

'Yes, I think we do,' agreed my mum, giving me a strange, wistful look. Sad almost.

Sue went over to the phone and lifted the receiver just as the kitchen door opened and Zeus slouched into the house looking like he had been in the bath.

'*Zeus!*' I went over and petted him, thinking that Ellie would walk in right behind him. She didn't. Nanny did.

'Me find this beast cryin' over near the park,' he said, shaking his head so that the rain flew off his dreads in every direction.

'Where's Ellie?' asked Mr Sykes. 'Was she with the dog?'

'I'm sorry, Brian – she wasn't.'

Nanny looked at all the faces in the kitchen and then cocked his head to the left, something he did when he was angry or, in this case, confused. 'Why? What's up?'

'Ellie's missing,' I told him. 'She went out with Zeus hours ago and she hasn't come back yet.'

Nanny just stood and stared at me. Then he looked

down at Zeus. 'The beast has been in a fight,' he said, pointing at Zeus' head. 'Him have blood 'pon him face.'

I had a closer look. There was a cut above one of his eyes and another deeper cut by his left ear.

'Oh my God!' Ellie's mum started to cry.

'Sue, call the police.' My mum's voice rang out over the kitchen like a foghorn. Clear and authoritative. She was the calmest one out of us all. Like she was used to situations like these. Which I suppose she was.

Sue was still holding the receiver. She put it down, picked it up again and dialled. 'Yes, I'd like the police please.'

Della started crying and Jas gave her a hug. I went over and stood by Mr Sykes, trying to stay calm, only my stomach was diving at an impossible speed, making me feel sick. My mum hugged Marge, telling her that everything would be all right. But Marge just stood and shook slightly, her bottom lip quivering.

'I'd like to report a missing person,' said Sue into the receiver. She stopped and thought for a second before continuing, 'I mean, a missing child . . .'

ten:
wednesday, 11.30 p.m.

The police took nearly an hour to come round. They spent a long time next door before Ellie's dad rang to say that the police wanted to talk to us. I was in the kitchen when I took the call, trying to stay calm. The rest of the Crew were in the living room with Nanny. No one was talking. There was an air of disbelief in the house. We had all seen this type of thing on the news or in a drama show on the telly, but it wasn't the kind of thing that we ever expected to happen to someone we knew. Not that we knew exactly what had happened to Ellie. We didn't. But it was hard not to fear the worst.

What about that weirdo she'd seen a few times? Was he a nonce? Or could it be connected with the money we'd found? Nah – we'd handed that in, so it couldn't be someone wanting that back.

I couldn't sit still. I spent the time waiting for the police by moving between the kitchen, the living room and my bedroom, all the while blaming myself for what had happened. If only I had given in to Ellie, like I normally did, and taken Zeus myself, none of this would have happened. She would be here now, moaning at me to take her to the cinema, dissing some lad at her school, or calling me a sad old man. I wanted to go back out to look for her, but where would I have gone? Who would I have spoken to? I went into the living room at one point and just stood by Della, looking at everyone in turn without saying one word. I didn't know what to say. Nanny was sitting in his favourite chair, a beaten-up leather thing that my mum had 'rescued' from the top of a skip and restored. He had a reggae CD playing at low volume and sat staring at nothing in particular. It felt like everyone, even Zeus who had retired to his basket in the kitchen, was numb. I suppose we were.

Two uniformed coppers turned up, along with a bloke in a suit who introduced himself as DI Griffin. They followed Ellie's dad into our kitchen, and one of the uniformed officers asked to speak to me, sitting down to take details. DI Griffin was talking to my mum and Sue, asking them who they were and explaining that he was part of a new unit that dealt with child abduction and paedophilia. As he asked them questions I could see that Sue was becoming agitated. I didn't hear exactly what he was asking but it must have been something that upset her.

DI Griffin eventually got round to me after asking everyone else individually about what they knew. Jas started to say that they were out of order, asking us all separately, as if we had concocted some cover story and they wanted to catch us out. 'Man, that ain't right. What – they sayin' we know something? That we done it?'

'It is a strange thing to do,' I said, thinking back to all the police crime series that I had seen on the telly. But then the TV was hardly real life, unless you were one of those sad people who thought *Big Brother* was about reality and cried when soap characters got married or died.

'It ain't strange, bro. It's out of order. They are making us out to be criminals and we're the ones that asked them for help.'

I didn't know what to say to that and before I could reply the policeman asked me into the kitchen. 'So, Billy. You were the last person to see Ellie.' It wasn't a question. It was a statement. Griffin, the DI, picked at his ear with a finger.

'Yeah, I was,' I said, trying not to stare as his little finger disappeared into his ear up to the knuckle.

'So, did she seem upset or worried about anything?' he said, pulling his finger out and wiping it on his trousers. The scutter.

'No, not really. She didn't wanna take Zeus for a walk but then she never does,' I said.

'And you and her didn't have a fight or an argument? Lovers' tiff, maybe?' This time he clasped his hands in front of him, staring into my eyes.

'You what?' I wondered what he was on about. What did he mean 'lovers' tiff'?

'Well . . . ?'

I stared straight back into Griffin's eyes. 'No, we never had no argument and we couldn't have had a "lovers' tiff" because we ain't lovers.'

'That's not the impression that we've been getting, son,' he said, unclasping his hands and picking his left ear with his right forefinger this time.

'I ain't no son of yours and I don't know where you get that impression but you're wrong,' I said angrily.

'Your friends seem to think you are a little bit fond of her . . .' He stared deeper into my eyes, trying to find some weakness. Trying to make me anxious.

'Yeah, yeah. I doubt they said that.'

'Maybe she doesn't feel like that about you. Maybe she's got another boyfriend. One . . . let's just say a boy less colourful than you . . .' With that he smiled, proud of himself.

'*You what?*' I couldn't believe what Griffin was saying.

'Well, you do have a previous record, son.'

'So? That makes me what, exactly . . . ?'

'Colourful.' This time he picked his right ear again, rolling up whatever he found between thumb and fore-finger and flicking it at the ground.

'You can't get away with that!'

'Calm down, son. I'm only ascertaining what you know.'

I was livid. I wanted to jump up and smack him in the mouth but my sense got the better of me.

'Your gang are a strange bunch, aren't they? Very mixed.'

'Yeah, and . . . ?'

'That's very strange for this area, isn't it? I mean, round here your blacks stick with blacks and your Asians with other Asians and white kids are few and far between.'

'That says more about how little you know than any-thing else,' I replied. 'And where would you put me, mate?'

'Well, you're a mixture, aren't you?'

'And . . . ?'

It went on for another twenty minutes, with Griffin asking me stuff that had nothing to do with Ellie's disappearance. It was as though he was trying to get me to say something that would incriminate me or wind me up. In the end I just gave him yes or no answers. I wanted to punch him but I stayed calm and let him carry on. I wasn't going to let him get the better of me.

The police left after Ellie's dad came round and gave them a recent photograph of her. They said they would send someone round within twenty-four hours to follow up. Ellie's dad went back to his house. Sue gave Jas and Will a lift home and I sat up with Nanny as he listened to various reggae CDs. I was really tired but I couldn't sleep. My mind played over and over, trying to think where Ellie could be. Who could have harmed her. I told Nanny about the way that DI Griffin had questioned me.

Nanny just smiled and nodded his head. 'What did you expect, Billy?'

'But I haven't done anything wrong.'

'Dem nah care about dat. Is a little white girl gone missing. That's all they care about. Not how you feel.'

'It ain't got nothing to do with her being white,' I said, confused.

'You don't think? Think about how many news stories you see 'bout children gone missing. How many of them stories are about black or Asian kids? How many news-paper campaigns you see about ethnic kids?'

'I've seen loads,' I said, lying. Nanny had a point. I'd seen a few recently but only after the stories had been taken up by the national press.

'Little black kid gone missing and you might see two, maybe three reports. White kid and you see the reports all day, every day for time. You see celebrity appeal 'pon television and newspaper set up campaign.'

'Yeah . . .'

'I man ain't saying that it all right to kill white kids or nothing like that. I just sayin' that every child have the same worth. Them colour nah matter. But it does to dem media and police. So dem nuh care if they hurt I feelings – or yours.'

'You don't think Ellie is dead, do you?' I shivered at the thought.

Nanny shook his head. 'Nah, man, I nuh say that. But we need to find her soon, man.'

'How are we gonna do that? The police are doing it anyway. And if you're right, cos she is white, they'll be doing everything they can to find her so that's good, isn't it?'

'Listen, from when she get kidnap in we neighbourhood then some man *mus'* know something. Man can't fart around here without someone hear it.'

'So what do we do?' I asked, getting up from my chair.

'*We* nah do nothing. I man will go ask some questions. Just let me get a little meditation. Help me think straight.'

And with that he sparked up a spliff and sat back, thinking. I wanted to tell him that I didn't think getting stoned would help but I didn't want a lecture about weed being a herb from Jah and how it was the healing of the nation. In fact I probably would have smoked some myself if I had stayed there. But I went up to my room and my own thoughts.

eleven:
five
days later...
monday

Ellie's parents made appeals on the local TV station and the radio on the second and fourth days after she had gone missing and the police liaison officer came by every day. They were desperate for some kind of news and each hour that passed without any word of Ellie saw them grow a little more anxious. They were normally a really happy family, making little jokes about each other and doing the kind of family stuff that me, Jas and Della had never done. Christopher, Ellie's brother, had this annoying habit of whistling the tune to *Lady in Red* by Chris De Burgh – that was his joke name, one his dad had given him to wind him up – and he had even stopped doing that. It was horrible to see them become so sad.

It was one of the worst periods of my life. I couldn't eat or sleep or stop thinking long enough to do anything at all. The Crew had been out asking questions of the local kids and gangs, me included, but we had gleaned no information at all. Apart from the message that I was given about Busta and how he was going to kill me and Della for 'dissin'' him. The message was delivered by two of Busta's gang, down an alleyway in their part of the ghetto. It was the local front line and I had been asking the kids around there about Ellie, trying to make sure that I avoided Busta. I didn't. As I was walking down an alley between two streets I found my path blocked by two lads. One of them had three teeth missing and hands like shovels. The other one was skinny but looked more scary than the big one. The alley was damp with the rain and it smelt of cat shit and rubbish. I had nowhere to run. The big one held me against a wall and the smaller one punched me in the face and stomach, delivered the message and then hit me again.

I must have passed out because I found myself waking up in a puddle, with a ginger tom cat licking my face. I got to my feet and slowly made my way home, helped part of the way by the local imam, the priest from the disused mosque at the back of the train station. He was a local man and I had seen him around for years. He asked me if I wanted to call the police but I told him to leave it. He shook his head and smiled kindly, before telling me that I was always welcome at the mosque when it eventually reopened, regardless of my religion. I smiled weakly back at him and walked into my house. As I entered the kitchen, relieved that my mum was at work, my phone started to vibrate in my pocket. It was Della.

'I'm fine,' I told Della as we sat in my kitchen. She had come straight round after her phone call and we were waiting for Jas to join us.

'We can't let Busta's crew get away with what they did,' she replied. She had been scowling since she'd arrived

72

but still managed to look pretty with it, something I had always found amazing. Man, Della was even pretty when she cried and there aren't many people you can say that about.

'We can't do anything. They've got serious back-up.'

'So just because they sell drugs, that means they can do what they like?'

I nodded. 'Since when has it been anything else round here, Dell?'

'It's lame, man. I feel we should just go and—'

'I'm fine. It ain't the first time I've had a beating and it won't be the last. Man, let it go. You and me better try and avoid Busta, but more importantly we need to find Ellie – that's all that I care about.'

'Yeah but . . .'

'Yeah but nothing. Where's Jas got to? Call him, will you.'

Della got out her phone and sent Jas a text message. Within a minute her phone bleeped at her in reply. As she read the message, Jas himself knocked on the kitchen door and walked in.

'Yo, what up with your face, man?' he asked, looking at me.

'Nothing. Just a little run in with Busta's boys.'

'So let's go and deal with them,' he replied angrily.

'Forget it, Jas. Let's concentrate on finding Ellie if we can.' I really couldn't be arsed with Busta and his crew – not when Ellie was missing. Man, I was missing her like mad.

'They ain't getting away with this, man. Believe.'

'It can wait,' I told him.

In hindsight I should have listened to Jas, but that's the

thing about hindsight. It's about as useful as a mobile phone with no charger.

We sat and talked about what we were going to do to help find Ellie. Jas had already been round and spoken to a couple of lads who liked her, just to see if they knew anything, but to no avail. Della had called all her friends at school and asked some of the local girls but none of them knew anything. I hadn't had any joy either. It was like Ellie had just disappeared from the face of the planet. No trace. But I was sure that someone knew something. Nanny had been right about how everyone round here knew everyone else's business. And then something hit me. Something that I'd dismissed earlier but which should have been obvious. I looked at Della.

'It's got to have something to do with the money,' I said, almost in a whisper. 'Ellie's disappearance.'

'What you on about, man?' Jas looked unconvinced. '*Ellie* didn't find it.'

'Yeah, and we gave the money back, Billy.'

'We gave it back to the police. Not to the actual owners.'

'The strange man that Ellie saw,' I went on. 'You and Will saw him too, man. They were watching us. And if Ellie saw *him*, he'd have seen *her*. What if they don't know we gave the money to the police, but reckon Ellie has it? Or me?'

'Oh shit,' said Della suddenly. 'The brick through your mum's window. That was the same night that we gave the dough back.'

'Exactly,' I replied.

It made sense. It was too much of a coincidence that we had found the money, handed it in and within days Ellie had disappeared.

'They might have followed us all at some point,' continued Della.

'And it isn't that hard to do. How many cars drive around these streets slowly? It's a red light area.'

Jas thought about it for a while before agreeing that I could have a point. Then he pointed out that, if I was right, then there was a criminal gang in the area that knew what was going on. Knew where Ellie was. And we couldn't just walk up to them and ask. So how were we going to find out which gang had Ellie – and why? We didn't have the money any more. Surely they'd know that by now? So why would they have taken her? It was a scary thought.

It was a thought that I passed on to Nanny later that day. He sat and listened before nodding slowly and telling me that I should be a copper, a suggestion that I took with the tonne of salt with which it was offered. He then asked me about the bruise that had appeared on my face and I told him about Busta and his crew.

'De yout' dem round 'ere is too feisty,' he said, shaking his head.

'It's cool, Nan. I'll deal with it after we've found Ellie.'

'Maybe you could leave Busta fe me to deal wid. I know a lickle ting 'bout that bwoi mek him cry with shame, y'know?'

I smiled. 'Man, is there anyone round here you don't know?'

'You forgetting, Sleepy. Before me find my callin' in Rastafari, I was doin' all dem t'ings that yuh see badman doin' now. I sell drug. I even hold a gun.'

'No way! You never told me that.'

'Well, is like yuh man Horace Andy a sing. Yuh see a man face but yuh can nevah see him heart.'

'You're telling me, man. Did you ever shoot anyone?' I asked.

But Nanny shrugged off my questions, telling me that he was talking about a man called Norris Grant, a man who had died long ago. Norris Grant was the name Nanny had been given at birth.

As we were talking my phone shrilled out its Mary-J ring tone and revealed Will on the other end of the line. He was out of breath and I assumed he had just finished at the gym but his voice gave the game away. Something was wrong.

'It's Jas . . . some lads got him and held him down . . .'

'Who?' I felt a chill run down my spine.

'He doesn't know. He just said that there were two lads and an older man. The older one told him to give back the other bag.'

'What other . . . ?' The first chill was joined by another.

'There were two, Billy. One that we handed to the coppers and *another* one . . .'

'What other one . . . ?'

twelve:
tuesday,
4.30 p.m.

'Are you sure you didn't see another bag, Will?'
The Crew had gathered at Will's house the next day. Jas was shaken but not hurt and he was angry – humiliated – because he was a kick-boxer and they had still got him. And he had been riding over to Della's on his skateboard, which they had broken. And the worst of it was that he didn't have a clue who had jumped him. It was getting a little hot for us, what with my run-in too. There was something weird going on and we had to figure out what it was. There had been no news of Ellie and the police hadn't found out anything either.

We were all playing the waiting game, hoping that something would give. That someone would come forward. At least my suspicions about the money had been confirmed, even if they hadn't been totally accurate. Whoever had left that money in the alley had left two bags, which meant that there was one still out there somewhere. And we were getting the blame for it. The money had to be linked to Ellie's disappearance. The warning that Jas had been given said as much. The question was what we were going to do about it. Were we supposed to go to the police or not?

'There was no second bag, man,' replied Jas. 'If there had been, we would have grabbed that too.'

'Yeah, why would we take one and not the other?' added Will.

Della looked at Jas and shrugged. 'I wish you hadn't grabbed that bag at all, Jas,' she said in a whisper.

'Yeah, so do I,' he replied, looking worried.

I told them that it was too late to worry about the money now. We had to come up with a plan of action.

'Well, we can forget the police for a start. They ain't exactly being helpful,' continued Della.

'But they can use the information to find Ellie,' argued Will.

'Yeah, and they can use the same information to give us more grief. I mean, they ain't stupid, are they? First we hand in a bag full of dough and then Billy's house gets attacked. And now . . . Ellie,' concluded Jas.

He was right. The police knew all about the bag of money we had found already, and the second bag didn't change that. It would just mean more interviews for us with DI Griffin and his ilk. After the way they'd treated us before – all nasty and sus – I knew they wouldn't believe us if we told them there was a second bag and we hadn't taken it. They'd think we had kept the second bag and would pressure us to give up money we never had. Worse still, it would probably mean they'd ease off on other ways to try and find Ellie. If it would have helped Ellie, we'd have been down there like a shot – Babylon or no Babylon – but there was nothing new that would help. Nah, it was up to us to decide what to do.

'Someone *has* to know something,' I said.

'Yeah, but who?' asked Jas.

That was the key question. It was obvious that who-ever had left that money in the alley had been watching us and knew that we had handed in a bag of money to the police. They also thought that we had another bag – but we didn't. However, if two bags *had* been left in the alley, then one of them must have been taken by some-one else – another gang or maybe even a wino or junkie. If we could find whoever that was, get the second bag and let it be known we had it, surely whoever had Ellie would come for it and we'd get Ellie back. After all, that's what the message to Jas meant, didn't it? The money for Ellie. Or we could let the police handle it. But they wouldn't want to give the second bag – if they found it – back to any owners. Not if it was dodgy money. I was sure of that.

Finding whoever had the second bag would be diffi-cult, regardless of whether it had been taken by another gang or some lucky individual who had happened to stumble across it. But then, if there *had* been two bags together, why hadn't the first person to see them taken both? It just didn't make sense. Who would leave all that money in an alley? And if we went to the police . . . Man, my thoughts were just moving round in one big circle.

We decided to split into two and go out again. Someone had to know *something*. Maybe a crew who had suddenly come into a suspiciously large amount of money recently?

This time Della and Jas went together and I stuck with Will. I told Jas to steer clear of the area round the front line, just in case Busta was about, and to keep a lookout for anyone suspicious – which could have meant a thousand people in our area. I didn't want him or Della to have another run-in with Busta. We didn't need any more complications. Will and I would go round the more dangerous parts of the neighbourhood, including the precinct by the community centre and the underground concrete car parks that sat at the base of every tower block, like ready-made lairs for modern-day Fagins. They housed young black, Asian or white lads withered by heroin and crack abuse, shadows that leapt out as you passed, sticking you with blades and taxing your mobile and money. It was like Victorian London transposed to modern British inner-city life. Only Oliver Twist was a junkie rent-boy who would beat and rob your granny – and brag about it to his crew.

It was cold out again, although at least it was no longer raining, and we made our way to the community centre, past the post office, an off-licence and a halal butcher's. Will stopped at the butcher's to talk to the owner's son, Mohammed, who was our age. Mo told Will that he had seen Ellie with Zeus on the day she had gone missing. But he had seen her coming out of the alley and that was it. He couldn't remember which way she had gone or if anyone was following her, either on foot or in a car. Will told me what Mo had said as we walked through the precinct and over to the community centre. A gang of kids were hanging around the entrance, boys and girls, smoking cigarettes and drinking from cans of strong lager. One of the girls gave me the eye as we walked in and then, when my back was turned, made a lewd comment about me and what she'd do to me if I'd let her.

I pretended not to hear but Will pounced on it. 'That

girl wants you, dread. You should go get her number.' He grinned at me.

'Maybe when she's legal,' I replied. The girl must have been all of fourteen going on twenty-one.

The centre had an inner hall that was a gym and indoor football pitch. It was used to stage reggae and ragga sound systems and garage nights at the weekend. I hadn't been a regular visitor for a couple of years but I knew the community worker who ran the place, Gary. He was yet another old friend of Nanny's and he shook his head when I asked if he had seen Ellie recently, telling me Nanny had been round already asking him that. I asked him if Busta's crew still dealt drugs outside and he shook his head about that too.

'We moved them on a few months ago – me, Nanny and a couple of other youth workers.'

'Bet that made him happy,' laughed Will, talking about Busta.

Gary just shrugged. 'No, it didn't. But all he did was move on up the road.'

'And no one else has been in asking about the gangs round here?'

'Funny you should mention that, Billy. The only other person who's been in is Nanny, as I said, and he was asking the same questions as you two. He told me about your friend. The missing girl that's been on the telly.'

'Oh, right.' I wondered what Nanny was up to. I almost expected him to come flying to the rescue wearing a cape and his underpants on top of red, gold and green tights, like a Rastafarian super-hero.

'You know, regardless of your feelings about the police – and they don't exactly ingratiate themselves with the

81

youths around here – you should let them deal with it. They have better resources and more people.'

'Yeah, but we've got the ghetto super-hero on our side,' I replied, grinning at my image of 'Nanny-man'.

Gary looked at me as if I was mad and shook his head. 'I hope you've not been eating those magic mushrooms again, Billy.'

Will laughed out loud. 'They ain't magic round here,' he said. 'Not unless you buy them from the man with the sweeties.'

. 'Hey, make sure you two leave the sweetie man alone,' replied Gary. 'There are enough sweetie fiends around here already.'

We said goodbye and left, heading for our next destination, the front line, home of the man with the sweets.

We turned up nothing about Ellie but thankfully we didn't bump into Busta or his gang either. The last thing we needed was more trouble. What we needed was a break. Jas and Della turned up at mine around half seven that evening. They'd had no luck. No one had seen Ellie or anyone else who might be suspicious. No one knew of anyone who had suddenly become loaded. They had spoken to lots of the younger kids who hung around the streets during the summer holidays. Nothing.

Looking at Della, I noticed that she had changed her clothes from earlier. I was getting to be a regular little Sherlock Holmes. 'You been home?' I asked her, not thinking too much of it. Della raised her eyebrows and then shot a glance at Jas. He looked away.

'Er . . . yeah. We . . . I mean, I had to change. I bought a drink and spilled it down my top.'

I looked at her and winked, nodding in Jas's direction. 'Naughty you.'

'What you trying to say?' she replied, but not angrily. She was smiling. Like a cat. Devious. I just laughed as Jas turned a shade of red that I didn't think it was possible for Asian people to turn.

And then I chastised myself for making jokes when things were so messed up. The Crew was one very important person short and we were going to move heaven and earth to find her, if that was what it took. We just had to continue asking around the ghetto. Someone must have seen Ellie. They had to have.

thirteen:

tuesday, 8 p.m.

We walked up towards the ring road that encircles the ghetto and followed it past Burger King and Kentucky Fried Chicken towards the city centre, before heading left towards Victoria Park on the outskirts of the centre. There was a long road that led to the park and it was full of takeaways, Indian restaurants, pubs and bars. There was also a sex shop, about five newsagents' and three off-licences. Along the way we stopped at a couple of taxi-cab offices and asked questions of the drivers. Nothing. Further up, outside a student pub we talked to a group of Asian lads who told us that they weren't from the city. They were in town to find accommodation for the new term, which was still a month and a half away. Again nothing.

Jas and I called in at one of the off-licences. The owner, Mr Sharma, was an old Asian man who had been there for years – we knew his kids. There was a poster tacked to his counter, a police notice about a recent robbery with an appeal for information.

'You had some trouble, Uncle-ji?' I asked, pointing but not really looking at the poster. They were a regular feature in most of the off-licences in the ghetto.

'Oh – you knowing, *beteh*. Nothing that bad.' He shrugged his shoulders.

'When was that?'

He sighed. 'Other night. Bloody kids, them, innit. Telling me they eighteen when they not even sixteen.' He looked out of the shop window and then at the door – as though he were expecting them to come back any minute.

'What did they steal? Money?'

'No, they not stealing money. Just kids, innit. They stealing few cans of beer.'

I shook my head. 'Were they local kids?'

''Course – always local ones doing worst. Bloody know the boy's name too. Divinder bloody Kooner. I even knowing his old man.' Mr Sharma shrugged again.

I thought about the name. It rang a bell. He was a local lad, about two years younger than me. Jas had had a ruck with him a while back over a dodgy mobile phone or something.

Then I saw the date on the poster. It was the same night that Ellie had gone missing. 'This happened last week? Last Wednesday? The same night as the girl went missing?'

'Girl in newspaper? Yes, same night. I opening paper next day, see if my shop mention, evening edition, and I'm seeing picture of young girl. Bad thing, that, *beteh*.' He shook his head slowly. 'Seen her too . . .' he added.

I looked at Jas and then straight at Mr Sharma. Result! 'You *saw* her? That night?'

'Yes. She walking bloody great animal up road. I think animal walking her . . .' he said, chuckling to himself.

'Look, Uncle-ji, it's really important. She's our friend. What did you see?' I was excited. Out of nowhere we had got a lucky break.

'I calling police and the lads start the running and I'm going out to street, behind them. Police car come quick and when the policemans get out, I point out Divinder to him. Divinder running up road past your friend but bloody police running in other direction, after other boys who not stealing anything. Bloody typical, innit?'

'And you *saw* Ellie?' I continued excitedly. Jas and Della had come into the shop by now and they were listening intently.

'Yes. She walking dog up towards park and then she take left. Gotham Street, I think. That Divinder, him running in same way.'

'Did you tell the police?' asked Della, beating me to it.

'They not bloody asking and they not coming back after they leaving the poster.'

I grinned at the rest of the Crew. 'Thanks, Uncle-ji,' I said as we left.

It was a break. A small break, but important all the same. What we had to do now was find Divy Kooner.

The precinct that Will and I had visited earlier in the day was now shuttered up, save for the off-licence. There was a crew hanging around outside the open shop – the kind of crew that, if you didn't know them, would probably make you think twice about going anywhere near them. There were about thirty kids in all, some of them drunk and one or two smoking weed. They were noisy and feisty but they were basically harmless. The shop itself was the kind where everything was behind glass and you had to ask the owner to fetch you what you wanted. It had been robbed at least five times that I could remember. The security measures were understandable.

The owner was another old Asian man, Mr Singh, and he worked there with two of his sons and kept a huge Alsatian dog for extra security. The thing was mad. Whenever anyone walked into the shop it would start to snarl and smash against the glass and Mr Singh would have to shout at it and hold it back.

We had already spoken to Mr Singh, so we didn't go in, but said hello to a few of the kids outside instead. Besides, we knew who we were looking for. Divy. And according to Jas he would be in the community centre, playing pool or chilling out. The centre stayed open until ten-thirty every night and as the day progressed so did the quality of its crowd. Downwards. There were some older lads standing around outside the doors – dealers waiting for their customers – and a couple of cars were parked to the side of the building.

Jas and Della went in to see if Divy was around while Will and me went around to the car park. He wasn't exactly hard to miss, Divy. Years of getting involved in other people's business and generally being too cheeky had left him with a boxer's nose, so flat that it might as well not be there. He was about my height and heavily built and his hair was cut into a fade like Jas's – only Divy had a red streak running through his. On the way over, Jas had joked that Divy's red streak should have been yellow.

As we walked round to the side of the building Will pointed at the occupants of one of the cars. It was two of Busta's crew. 'Right, let's see how brave they are when the numbers are even, man,' he said, moving towards the car.

I grabbed Will and held him back. We didn't need any more trouble. 'Leave it. We're here to find Divy. They can wait till later.'

Will grinned. 'Don't worry, Billy. I only wanna play with them.'

He pushed me aside as though I weighed nothing and walked up to the car, kicking the driver's side door as he reached it. The door crumpled slightly – enough to leave a costly dent. It flew open and the smaller of the two lads who had beaten me up got out. Will started to grin – only his grin was kind of sardonic.

'Yo! Yo! What the raas . . . ?' began the driver.

He didn't finish because Will grabbed his leading arm and twisted it behind his back, making him cry out in pain. Then he leaned in close to the lad's face. 'Never mind messages fe my Crew. Tek one fe Busta. Tell him I never like his ugly face from school. And now I ain't no nine-stone weakling him can push around, unnerstand? Tell him Will says hello.'

'I . . . I . . . I'll tell him, man. Leggo my arm – you're gonna break it, man . . .' His voice was unnaturally high-pitched for his age.

'Tell him we got a lickle problem, me and my Crew – but when we done with that, he's next. Yuh gets me?'

He released the lad's arm. The lad took a step back and began to rub his arm. And then bravado began to return to his face. 'I got it. But trust me, bad bwoi – you is getting messed up, man. Busta ain't—'

As he spoke Will took a step towards him and he shut up, cowering again as bravado went back to where it had come from.

'Just tell him,' growled Will.

And with that he turned and headed back towards where I was standing, watching. As he approached a chorus of shouts erupted behind me and then the sound of Jas's voice, swearing. I turned to see Divy Kooner running through the precinct shops towards the main road, trying to get away.

I looked at Will, who shrugged his shoulders and then grinned at me. 'What the hell, man. Be like lions chasing down their prey,' he said.

'You what?' I shouted, as we set off after Divy.

'*Fun!*' roared Will as we ran.

The kids by the off-licence whooped and shouted and cheered as we ran past them and on to the main road, turning left and heading for the streets round where we lived. Divy was out of sight but I saw Jas run over the road and turn right, down a side street, with Della in hot pursuit. Will cut across the road ahead of me, narrowly avoiding an oncoming car. I waited for it to pass before I followed.

The side street we ran into went up a hill towards an adventure playground and park at the top. It was narrow, cars parked on both sides, and ahead of me I saw Jas again, gaining on Divy, with Della being caught up by Will. My lungs were aching. I saw Divy turn right into another side street, closely followed by Jas. There was a street to the right, ahead of me, which would lead me in the same direction. I took it and ran up towards the park. It was a cobbled street, pedestrianized. The incline was less steep too and I knew that if I reached the top before Divy crossed ahead of me, we had him.

But just as I got to the top he raced past me, avoiding my attempt to lunge at him. Jas flew by a second later and I caught him instead, both of us hitting the ground. We got up quickly and went on but Divy was nowhere to be seen. Will and Della caught us up and we stopped for a moment.

'Where is he?' demanded Will.

'Lost him. This dick here . . .' Jas told him, pointing at me . . . 'knocked me over.'

'Nice . . . so where do we go now?'

'I was *trying* to catch Divy. I just missed him, that's all.' Well, I had to defend myself, although I did feel like a right idiot.

Della was standing with her hands pressed to her sides, taking deep gulps of air, trying to catch her breath. She began to say something and then coughed for about a minute.

'Yo, sister, looks like you need to come down the gym with me,' laughed Will.

'What? So I can come check out all those muscle Marys in their little shorts?' She shook her head. 'And don't smile, William. We just lost that ugly bwoi.'

Will stopped smiling and cursed Della under his breath.

'Let's not squabble, kids,' I said, trying to take control. 'He's gotta be around here somewhere.'

Jas raised his eyebrows. 'Nah, he's long gone, man.'

As he spoke we heard some dustbins rattle down the side passage of a house. It might have been a rat. Maybe someone's pet. But it wasn't. It was Divy. He had been crouching behind two large bins and something had obviously spooked him. And then I saw the biggest rat I have ever seen come hopping out from the passage and across the road to the cover of some bushes. Della shrieked and Will nearly jumped onto me. I laughed at them, telling them it was only a rat before turning to find that Jas had pinned Divy against the passage wall and was slapping him gently around the face. Playing with him like a cat with a mouse.

fourteen:

tuesday -
and wednesday

In the end Divy couldn't really tell us very much about Ellie and why she had disappeared. He did say, though, that he had seen a metallic green Saab driving up and down the road on the night she had gone missing. He had noticed it while he was hanging around by Mr Sharma's off-licence. In itself it wasn't that much of a lead, although it was suspicious. Most of the dealers around the area drove souped-up sports cars with blacked-out windows and big tyres – something I could never understand. I mean, they might as well have put a big neon sign on their cars – DRUG DEALER, THIS WAY PLEASE.

The thing was, the car that Divy had described wasn't one that any of us had ever seen around the streets. Generally we knew who drove which car, locally. Everyone did. The only ones we didn't know were those that belonged to the kerb-crawlers. But it hadn't been a hot summer night either – not with all that rain – certainly not hot enough to warrant driving around the streets like most of the lads here did whenever the sun came out, whistling at any girls they passed. So why would a car be driven around, again and again? Divy had seen it pass by at least ten times that night. In that weather, it had to be some desperate kerb-crawler looking for a girl.

Or someone else. Looking for one of us.

'Come on, man,' urged Jas when we got home. 'It *is* a lead – like in them crime novels that you read, Billy.'

'Man, you read *enough* of them,' added Will.

I thought about what my crime novel heroes would do in our situation. What would Matt Scudder and John Rebus and Dave Robicheaux do? Go to their police contacts, pay a snitch for information, lean on someone for a clue. But we didn't have their options. We weren't really detectives. We were a bunch of teenagers looking for our friend and hoping that she wasn't dead – we were *playing* at being detectives. We didn't have their contacts, their powers and we weren't characters on the pages of a crime novel. We were real and we didn't have a chance.

I started to get angry. 'This ain't a novel, Jas. This is real. We ain't the sodding Famous Five!'

The rest of the Crew looked at me in surprise. I hadn't realized how abruptly I had spoken.

'This is real effing life and our friend is out there somewhere and we don't know whether she is alive or dead and all we can do is pretend we are detectives and sit around listening to CDs!'

Della looked startled and Jas lowered his head. Will whistled silently. I waited for a moment and felt a hot tear fall down my cheek. And then I said sorry.

Della leaned over and gave me a hug. 'It's all right, Billy,' she said, wiping my face.

'No it ain't,' I replied. 'Ellie ain't here. We should have

looked out for her. We should have . . . I should have taken that bloody animal out myself. It's my fault.'

'No, it's not. You didn't know what would happen. We don't know what *has* happened.'

'Come on, Dell,' I continued. 'How many times do we see this shit on the telly. It might have *nothing* to do with the money. Girls go missing and no one sees them and then they turn up in a ditch five months later . . .'

Della looked to Jas for support but all he did was sit and stare. Will got up and left the room.

'Look, Billy, we are all upset here,' she said finally. 'I ain't slept since my Baby went missing. I wanna cry and I wanna hit someone and I wanna scream, but who is that going to help?'

I looked into her catlike eyes.

'It don't help anyone if we shout at each other and sit and feel sorry for ourselves. We are doing what we can and it may not be enough and we might only be kids but I ain't losing another member of my family. I done that too many times already.'

I hugged her back and then Jas joined in.

It was like we had all just bottled up our real feelings and as each day passed we had grown more and more tense. Until that point. I was missing Ellie and I was scared and upset and angry but Della was right. We were all feeling it and we weren't helping matters by sitting around moaning about it. I got up and went downstairs to find Will. He was in the living room, leafing through a paper. I went in and looked at him.

He just nodded. 'I know, man,' he said. 'I know.'

And then I began to feel guilty for calling Zeus 'that bloody animal'. I went into the kitchen and saw him sitting in his basket. He had hardly moved since that night and he still hadn't eaten properly. In fact he actually looked ill. I went over and knelt down to pet him. He whined a couple of times and then licked at my hand.

'Hey, kid,' I told him, 'it wasn't your fault, was it? It wasn't mine either. You missing Ellie, kid?'

Zeus shifted his head at the mention of her name and then he whined some more. I was crying again and petting him.

'I know, Zeus . . . I miss her too.'

The police came back round to Ellie's the following evening – one week now since Ellie's disappearance – and my mum went next door to be with Ellie's parents. They said they'd had no luck finding her. Ellie's mum was distraught and her dad had taken time off work to stay at home. When my mum got back she made a big pot of chickpea curry, telling me that maybe someone could take some over to Ellie's parents when it was made.

'They can't live on takeaway food,' she said. 'And Ellie's mum can't cook at the moment.'

I nodded slowly.

'Will you take it to them later, Sleepy boy?' she asked as she stirred the pot.

'Yeah, 'course I will, Mum. I want to go and see how they are anyway.'

'Thanks, Billy. How are you today?'

She came over and put her arm around me. I told her about how I'd felt the day before and she told me that Della was right.

'I know it's really hard for you all but we have to be

strong for Ellie's parents and for Christopher,' she told me.

I smiled a bit. 'You mean Chris De Burgh?' I said, trying to cheer up a bit, only it didn't work.

'Yes, for everyone.'

'It's just hard, Mum.'

'I know. And the longer she stays missing, the harder it will be, baby. But you've got to have hope.'

I looked at my mum, at her kind face, and I wanted to cry again. How was I supposed to have hope when the police had found nothing? When no one had seen anything? Even Mr Sharma and Divy hadn't really helped.

And then I knew. We *had* to tell the police what we had been told about a second bag. We had to. We could be holding what might be important information about Ellie from them. What if it stopped them from finding her?

I thought about telling my mum about it first but she didn't give me a chance.

'Have you seen Nanny?' she asked me.

I shrugged. I hadn't seen him for a day or so. 'No,' I replied. 'Where is he?'

My mum looked at me kind of funny. 'I don't know. Maybe he's out asking after Ellie. You know, I did wonder whether her disappearance had something to do with that money you lot found.'

I swallowed and looked away, knowing that my mum would notice. But she chose to ignore it.

'And then I decided that I was being silly. You gave it in anyway, so the police know all about it. They'd know if it was connected, surely.'

'Er . . . yeah. I kind of thought about that too,' I said, remembering the warning Jas had been given. I really wanted to tell my mum about that but something stopped me and I didn't know what it was. Maybe I just didn't want to worry her any more. After all, we'd figured out the police probably wouldn't be able to do anything different, even if they did know about the second bag, but the threat on Jas must mean all the Crew were now at risk. Even me. More info than my mum needed right now, I reckoned. Everything in my head was going haywire anyway. I was trying hard to think positively but feelings of dread kept on taking over, making me want to cry. I swallowed again, then told my mum I was going to watch telly for a bit.

'OK,' she replied, smiling. 'I'll shout when the food's ready to take next door.'

'Cool.'

Around eleven that night I was sitting at the kitchen table reading a crime novel by James Lee Burke and drinking some of my mum's beer. I was trying to think of something other than Ellie but the words on the pages of the book were blurred and jumpy and I kept closing my eyes and seeing her sitting opposite me, asking me to help her with her homework or moaning about something and nothing, like she always did. The beer was making my head feel light and I fancied a cigarette. As Mum was upstairs, I found some of hers and took one outside into the yard.

Zeus got up from his basket when I opened the door and followed me outside. I messed about with him as I smoked, then threw the fag away. I hated the fact that I had started smoking and become addicted to it. But not enough to give up, Ellie always told me. She'd tell me that kissing me would be like sucking on an ashtray and she had a point too. Not that she'd ever kissed me. Right at that point I would have given up smoking on the spot to know she was safe, and I could give her a kiss and a hug, fag breath or no.

Zeus went down the yard towards the alley door. Suddenly he turned and ran back towards me, barking. I was so shocked to see him running that I didn't even stop to think about why he was barking. He started to bark in the direction of the alleyway. I told him to be quiet but as usual he ignored me. And then I heard a noise coming from the alleyway. I ran into the house and picked up a rolling pin before going back outside, towards the alley door. I raised the rolling pin above my head, edged towards the door slowly and lifted up the catch. The door would have creaked if I had opened it slowly, so I took a deep breath and pulled it open in one go. I saw a male figure in front of me in the dark, and I brought down the pin, catching sight of Nanny's face and hair a split second before I hit him with it, pulling it away.

'MAN, WHA' DE RAAS YUH DO!?' he shouted. There was a girl by his side.

'Nanny,' I said, taking a breath. 'Shit . . .'

'Who yuh think it would be – Frankenstein, man?'

The girl looked scared and ill. I could tell straight away that she was a working girl – not much older than me. I gave Nanny a look that said, Why are you creeping down the alley with a working girl?

He read my thoughts as usual. 'Chill out nuh, man,' he said. 'Me nah *buy* she time. This is Sally an' she have somethin' to tell we.'

fifteen:

wednesday

I could hear the drip, drip, drip of a leaking tap coming from the bathroom. The room I was in was cold and damp and the girl they had looking after me was gone. I didn't know exactly how many days I had been locked in that room, either tied to a chair or to a pipe near this dirty, smelly old mattress. It was hard to tell because I had been blindfolded all the time apart from when the girl took me to the bathroom or felt sorry for me and let me look around at my surroundings. The room was stripped bare, with rough plaster on the walls and holes in the ceiling and floor. There were electric wires hanging out everywhere and the window had been boarded up. It was a hell hole, but then I felt like I was in hell.

I had spent the first few hours — I don't know how many exactly — crying and shaking with shock. At first I thought that I was going to die but after what felt like a day or two I realized that if the man was going to kill me he wouldn't have left the girl with me to become a witness. The skinny girl . . .

The man who kidnapped me had been in and out of the room four or five times since putting me there, telling me that he hoped my friends would see sense and give back the second bag. He told me that someone had sent them a message. I had protested to

99

him, telling him that they had given the bag to the police and that there had only been one bag. But he had just laughed.

I couldn't see him through the blindfold but I could smell the strange mix of body odour and cheap aftershave that was his scent. He threatened to do horrible things to me and twice he had come so close to me that I could feel his breath against my skin. I wanted my dad to come and knock down the door and rescue me and I wanted Billy and Nanny and Jas and Will to hold my captor down so that I could kick the old pervert in his head and . . .

I spent a lot of the time wondering how and when they would rescue me. I had to keep on believing that they would because without that hope I would have just curled up and died and I wasn't about to do that. I asked the girl about the man who had kidnapped me but she was too scared to talk. She told me that he would let me go soon and that I should keep calm and not make him angry. She told me that he got very violent when he got angry and that he was under a lot of pressure because we had taken money that he was supposed to get. At one point she mumbled his name but I didn't hear it clearly. I asked her if he was her boyfriend but she just shook her head and told me that girls like her didn't have boyfriends. Mostly, she said, they didn't have friends. She was really young too. Probably only about fifteen – a year older than me. She told me all about what she did too, a working girl. A child prostitute. It made me cry.

She asked me if I was OK, which really has to go down as one of the most stupid questions I've ever been asked and I told her so. But that made her cry and I could see that she didn't want to be there and that she had no part in what was happening to me so I talked to her some more. When she stopped crying, I told her that the only way that I could remain calm was to fantasize about who was going to rescue me and how they would do it. In the end I told her that my favourite rescue involved Angelina Jolie as Lara Croft, with the old pervert getting his head kicked in and Angelina doing her English accent bit. Absolutely.

And then I told her that I was thinking about what I would eat when I got out of there. I told her about my mum's roast dinners and Sue's vegetarian Thai stir fries and the omelettes that my dad made and Nanny's curries. I told her about Billy and how he had rescued me that first time and how much I missed my mum and then I cried . . .

I wanted my mum and dad. I wanted to hear Christopher whistling Lady in Red while I was trying to watch Hollyoaks. I wanted to call Billy an old man and I wanted Della to call me sister and Jas to tease me about how much he thinks I fancy Billy, and Will to lecture me about stuff . . . and I missed that stupid dog too. I carried on crying. The girl started crying too, saying she was sorry. Then suddenly she stopped and told me that she was going to help me get out. I said that she could untie me but she just ran out of the room and I was left all on my own . . .

sixteen:
wednesday, 11.30 p.m.

Nanny went to get my mum as I made the girl, Sally, a cup of tea. She sat at the kitchen table and held the mug in her hands and her eyes kept shifting from the mug to the door to the telly and back again. She was a little shorter than me and her hair, a honey blonde colour, was greasy and messy. She looked like she hadn't taken her make-up off for a few days; there were dark hollows around her eyes and if I could have seen her arms I knew that I would probably see needle-tracks. She caught me looking at her and tried to smile but it came out all lopsided and wrong and then she got embarrassed and turned away again. I asked her what she had to tell us but, without looking, she shrugged and said that she was waiting for Nanny to come back.

'He's nice, Nanny – isn't he?' she said, picking up her mug.

'Yeah, he's cool. How do you know him?' I replied, shocked at her voice, which was actually quite posh.

'I don't really – he's just one of those characters that you see about, you know? A bit like dealers and punters . . .' Her eyes glazed over and she got this distant look in them.

'So you're . . . what? A working girl?'

She smiled at my choice of words. 'Working girl? That's sweet.'

Sweet? I felt about five years old — again — and this time it wasn't even my mum making me feel that.

'Most of the kids around here call us slags and whores. You chose a very interesting way to put it.'

'Well, I have my reasons and the fact that I'm not a kid might help too,' I said, noticing for the first time the bruising around her neck. I had thought it was dirt but it wasn't.

'Where has Nanny gone?' she asked, looking right at me.

This time I looked away, realizing that I'd been staring at her. 'Erm . . . I think he's talking to my mum.'

'Your mum's called Rita, isn't she?'

'Yeah. How do you know that?'

Sally drank some more tea and then set the mug down on the table. 'She runs the drop-in centre. All the girls know who she is.'

'Oh right — of course.' I wondered why she did what she did and whether she really was as posh as she sounded. I had never met a working girl who spoke the way she did. Most of them had the local accent and swore loads and stuff. She was different.

I had to ask. 'Why do you do . . . ?'

'What I do?' She picked up the mug. 'Because I have a son and a flat and I can't survive on the money that I get from the government. Isn't that a bit of a cliché?'

'A bit — but if it's true . . . ?' She didn't look old enough to have a kid. But then a lot of young girls round here weren't old enough and they had kids.

'My son is two and I'm eighteen and . . . well, what else do you want to know?' She looked right into my eyes again.

'I don't know. I don't want to be nosy,' I replied.

'Yes you do. Ask me what you like. My customers are always telling me that I have a way of talking to them . . .' She looked away.

'So who is looking after your son now?'

'His grandmother.'

'You mean your mum knows what you do?'

'His father's mother. Not mine.'

'Oh.' I felt stupid again.

'My parents don't want me or my son because my son is mixed race.'

'So where's his dad?'

'Busy being a cliché in prison.'

I thought about asking her another question but she started to talk without any prompting from me.

'My son, Josh, is asleep at my flat with his grandmother looking after him. His dad is half black and half white and I suppose that makes Josh . . . well, how would you say it? I would just say he's a baby, not a colour, but you know how things are . . .'

'So what about your . . . ?'

'Parents? My dad supports the BNP and he told me that I would be polluting the English race if I had a "mongrel" child.'

'He called your son a mongrel?' I was incensed.

'No, he called my unborn baby a mongrel. My mum agreed with him and there you go. I left home, moved in with Josh's father and now it's just Josh and me. And his grandmother.'

'I'm mixed race,' I said, as though that would make the situation easier. It didn't.

'You ever heard that song by UB40, *The Pillow*?' she asked me.

'UB40? Nah. Bit ancient for me. My mum loves them, though.'

'Well, I swapped my dreams of shining knights,' she said, suddenly looking sad, 'for pushers, bars and money fights.'

'Is that from a tune of theirs?' I asked her. She nodded. 'Which CD is it on? I bet my mum's got it.'

She told me and then went back to her tea, which she finished.

'Do you want some more?' I said, wondering what was taking my mum and Nanny so long.

'Yes, please. What's your name anyway?'

'Billy.'

'I'm Sally,' she told me, although I already knew.

'Is that your real name?' I thought she might use a false name. My mum had.

'Yes. No point hiding behind a false name. This is the real me, bruises and all.'

I felt embarrassed. She must have noticed that I had been staring at her throat. 'You don't have to say where they're from,' I said.

'I wasn't about to.'

She put her fingers through her hair and I realized exactly how pretty she was and also how well it was hidden. Then she started singing softly.

'You've got a really good voice,' I said, but she ignored me and looked down at her mug.

'Where's my fresh mug of tea?' she said, not changing her gaze.

My mum came into the kitchen with Nanny five minutes later. She went straight over to Sally and sat down next to her, talking to her in a whisper and ignoring me and Nanny as though Sally was the only other person in the room. I suppose it was what my mum did and she was good at it. They spoke for about ten minutes and then my mum turned to me and Nanny.

'We should call the police,' she said.

I looked at Nanny but all he did was shrug.

'Call the *police* – why . . . ?' I asked, confused.

'Sally knows where Ellie is being kept,' answered my mum.

My heart jumped. 'Where . . . ?' I demanded, looking straight at Sally. She shrugged and looked at Nanny. 'Well . . . is someone going to tell me?'

Nanny did. Sally had been approached by a friend of hers, a young girl called Claire who was being forced to keep an eye on Ellie. The young girl had begun to have second thoughts and was scared that the kidnapper might hurt Ellie, so she had passed on Ellie's whereabouts to Sally, telling her to find Nanny. Sally trusted Nanny to deal with it without her or Claire getting officially involved – neither could afford to upset the man who had Ellie as they didn't know who he was working for. It could be some real bad man.

'WHERE IS SHE?' I shouted. I didn't want to wait for the police. They would take too long to get their shit together. They always did. And then I found out.

'In that *empty house*? Down the end of the street? THIS STREET?'

'Yes,' said Sally quietly.

I shook my head. We had been all over the ghetto looking for her and asking questions and all the time she had been held not a hundred metres from us. I started to get angry and I looked at Nanny for support. 'You're the one that tells me about how untrustworthy Babylon is. She's down the end of the fucking street and they haven't found her! I ain't waitin' fe dem – I'm going to get her. MYSELF!'

My mum stood up and grabbed my arm. 'Billy, leave it alone. It's up to the police. They know what to do. I've told Sally we'll keep her name out of it – we'll say we just had an anonymous phone call from some girl who heard we were asking around.'

'But she's there . . . now! Right now! And we're all standing around doing nothing.'

'I'll call the police now,' answered my mum but I wasn't listening.

'Call who you like – I'm going to get her. Nanny, you coming?'

Nanny pulled his dreads through his hands, like he always did just before he was ready to leave the house, but my mum shot us both a stare, then she shook her head slowly. 'Billy, the man who kidnapped Ellie could be there. He might hear you coming. He might hurt her.'

'He won't be there,' said Sally.

I looked at her, followed by my mum and Nanny. 'What?' we said in unison.

'Claire told me.'

I smiled. Nanny was straightening his hair again. 'So is jus' Ellie an' dis gal, Claire, in deh?' he asked Sally.

'Yes, I think so,' replied Sally. 'Look, I've gotta go. I can't hang around and talk to the police. I've done what

I can, but you don't need me any more.' She looked really scared, but at the time I ignored it.

I went over to her and kissed her on the cheek. 'Thank you,' I said as I turned and ran out of the kitchen door. 'And don't worry, I won't drop you in it.'

'BILLY!'

I didn't hear my mum, though. I had already gone into Ellie's yard and was knocking on her parents' back door. I heard someone enter the kitchen and then a light came on. Ellie's dad opened the door.

'Billy? What the hell . . . ?' He looked as though he hadn't slept for days and his eyes were red. I soon cheered him up though.

'Mr Sykes . . . I know where she is. I know where Ellie is!'

I told him what we'd found out – without mentioning Sally – and he said, 'Thank God!' and then ran inside again, coming back within a minute, wearing his shoes and holding a huge spanner. We rejoined Nanny in our back yard. When my mum came out and saw the look on Ellie's dad's face she suddenly realized that I was right. We had to go there – now!

Mr Sykes told her to call the police. To tell them that he was going to get his daughter and if the police didn't like it they could stuff it. Nanny grinned.

I followed Nanny and Mr Sykes out of the house and down the alley to the empty house at the end, picking up a spade that Nanny had left by the alley door.

seventeen:
thursday, 00.15 a.m.

The old empty house sat in total darkness. In the distance I could hear the sound of police sirens wailing and I wondered if they were heading in our direction. I was excited and scared at the same time, hoping that the kidnapper really wasn't in the house with Ellie. Ellie's dad smashed the glass in the window by the door, the window I had already partially broken, then reached inside to try and open the door but it wouldn't budge and he cut himself on a shard of glass. I asked him if he was OK but he ignored me and started to kick the door instead. The door creaked and groaned and little bits of wood splintered off it and flew up into the darkness. I told Nanny to help him kick it down and Nanny obliged, booting the frame. But it still didn't open.

I thought about climbing in through the broken window but there were still shards of glass sticking out of the frame and I didn't want to cut myself even worse than Mr Sykes had.

'Billy, give me that spade,' said Ellie's dad. 'I'll try to weaken the door frame.'

I handed it to him and he tried to force it between the

door and the jamb, splintering more wood as he did so. The door creaked and groaned some more, then it began to give. Nanny started to kick at it again as Ellie's dad pushed his body weight through the spade handle. Behind me, an animal of some sort scurried into the night and I turned to see what it was. In the distance, towards the street end of the alley, I thought I could make out a figure – a man. I told Nanny that someone was out there but he didn't stop kicking the door, which was finally beginning to yield.

I ran down the alley towards the man, suddenly scared that I didn't have any kind of weapon with me. I needn't have been. The figure saw me coming and turned and ran. As I got to the street he had turned into our road and I followed him, reaching the front of my mum's house just in time to hear the squeal of tyres from a metallic green Saab that was speeding away. I tried to get a look at the driver – or his two passengers – but I couldn't make out faces, only shapes. I didn't get time to read the numberplate either. I turned, intending to make my way back down the alleyway, then I realized that I could try the front of the house. It looked like whoever had kidnapped Ellie had just driven off in the opposite direction anyway. I started to run, hearing the wail of sirens get closer and closer . . .

I was sitting on a chair with my blindfold off, talking to the girl who had been left to look after me. She had told me that her name was Claire and I was talking to her about what she did and who she did it for. She wasn't really telling me anything at all. I think she was a bit shy, but mostly she was really scared. She wouldn't tell me who had kidnapped me. All she'd said was that she had sorted it all out and that she would be in really big trouble. She was shaking as she spoke. I just wanted to get out of that place and even though she had told me that she'd let someone know where I was, I didn't really believe her because she could just as easily have untied me and let me go herself. I told her so and she said that I was stupid. I mean, how nice is that? And to think that I had felt sorry for her.

Then she started crying and said that she was dead. 'He's gonna kill me when he finds me,' she said, between sobs.

I asked her who she was talking about but she didn't tell me. All she kept on saying was that we didn't understand, any of us, and that she wished she had just done what he'd said and not gone and told her friend Sally all about what was happening and where I was being held. She told me that she was the stupid one and that she was going to have to move to another city because she would get into real trouble here.

'He can't be that terrible, this man,' I said, realizing straight away that it was a stupid thing to say.

'He had you kidnapped, didn't he? He don't care. You don't understand.'

She did have a point. I was sitting there, thinking about who this girl Sally was and why telling her would have helped me to be rescued, when I heard what sounded like glass breaking from somewhere in the house. And then from somewhere else I heard a voice, his voice, shouting for Claire and swearing.

'You effing slag! Claire! Wait till the boss finds out about this! You're dead, you slag!'

I heard a door slam shut and then Claire started to pace about the room, mumbling to herself and rubbing her arms. 'I'm dead . . . I'm dead,' she kept on saying to herself. I tried to talk to her, to calm her down, but she suddenly turned and came over and glared at me, her eyes looking like they were on fire.

111

'You bitch! It's all your fault! You and your crew and now I'm gonna get killed 'cos of you, you slag!'

And then she hit me before running out of the room and down some stairs. I just sat there for about a minute, confused and scared and then I burst into tears. I screamed at her, over and over. 'I HATE YOU! I HATE YOU! I WANT MY DAD . . . PLEASE, I WANT MY DAD!

As I was crying I heard the sound of wood splintering and feet on a wooden floor coming from downstairs. I tried to stop crying and listen and I was sure I could hear my dad's voice and some-one else too and I started to cry some more, thinking that I was just imagining my dad's voice. Then I heard someone coming up the stairs from the other side of the house, then more people, and from outside the sound of police sirens. Suddenly my dad's voice rang out, for real, shouting for me and I called out myself and the footsteps got closer and closer and then I saw Billy come running through the door and then my dad and Nanny too. I burst into tears as Billy untied me, jumping into my dad's arms, kissing him and hugging him and then I let go and turned to Billy and I hugged him too and then . . . and then . . . I kissed him. And after that all I could do was cry . . .

. . . The front door of the house opened as I approached it and a young girl, who I assumed was Claire, the one who Sally had told us about, came running out in hysterics. I tried to stop her but she scratched my face and ran off down the street. I let her go. I was only interested in finding Ellie. I ran into the house and took the stairs three at a time when I heard Ellie's voice from upstairs.

She was in the room at the very back and I made my way towards her, slowly at first. The floor had boards missing and I didn't want to fall through it. I wouldn't be much use as a rescuer if I broke my neck falling through a dodgy floor. Behind me I heard Mr Sykes call out again and I looked over the banister, down the stairs and saw him at the bottom, Nanny right behind him.

'Up here!' I shouted.

Both of them ran up the stairs and followed me as I walked across the floor, stepping from joist to joist. The house was falling apart, with bare plaster and cracked walls and holes in the ceiling and floor. I felt so happy and so angry at the same time. I was going to see Ellie again! But I also wanted to kill whoever had kidnapped her and locked her up.

From outside I heard the sirens, on our street now, and then the sound of a copper's voice, followed by another, followed by yet another. I ignored them and stepped onto some sound floorboards and then ran through the door to the room where Ellie was. She was tied to a chair in the middle of the floor and she was crying. I knelt to untie her hands and feet, and as I finished she sprang up and jumped at her dad. My heart leapt. She was sobbing and hugging her dad and he was kissing her on the head and holding her tight. I turned to Nanny, who just stood by the door with a huge smile on his face, as if to say, 'Job done.' I winked at him and then turned to face Ellie, just as she threw her arms round me and started to cry even more. I hugged her tight and kissed her on the forehead.

'It's all right, Baby,' I told her, in a whisper. 'You're gonna be fine. We've got you. We've got you.'

She looked at me and I felt like crying too, as I watched the tears flowing down her cheeks and then . . . and then she kissed me.

I looked away and then back at her. She gave me a

funny look and then turned back to her dad as the coppers came through the door, like a speck of rain after a year of drought. The first one in was a uniform but he was followed by another, a blonde woman in a grey suit.

'What's going on here?' she said, looking from Nanny to me to Mr Sykes to Ellie. 'Looks like the private cavalry got here before us.'

eighteen:

thursday, 00.30 a.m.

The police took us to the Central Station to ask us questions about how we had found out where Ellie was. They asked me and Nanny the same questions over and over again. How did we know where she was? Who had told us? There was no way we'd drop Sally in it and Mr Sykes told them what we had told him – that we had been called by an anonymous girl who had tipped us off, having heard that we'd been asking questions in the neighbourhood. She hadn't given us her name. We'd told him and all he knew was that his daughter was being held not a hundred metres away and what would they have done in the same situation?

The CID officer who questioned us was a woman called Lucy Elliot and she described what had happened as 'a little bit irregular'. In the end though, despite her doubts about our tale, we were allowed to go home. After all, Ellie was safe. And what could Elliot say? That her colleagues were so useless that they hadn't even bothered to check an empty house at the end of our street?

It was so wicked to see Ellie and her family all together again – even 'Chris de Burgh' – and Ellie was overcome with emotion. I don't think she stopped crying from the minute we found her to when she finally went home and to bed.

Nanny and I left Ellie and her family in their kitchen and went home. I didn't go straight to bed, even though it was so late. When Nanny and I got in, my mum was waiting up with a cup of tea for us. She gave me a kiss on the forehead, saying, 'Well done!', then asked us what had happened and what the police had said. I asked her where Sally had gone.

'Home. To her son. She said to tell you thanks for not telling the police she was involved,' said my mum.

'How did she know that I wouldn't?' I asked, before sipping at my tea.

'She trusted us, baby.' My mum smiled.

'Oh,' I replied, through a yawn.

'She said that she'd see you around sometime,' continued my mum. 'You certainly seem to have made an impression on her.' My mum was being sly. Trying to be funny. Thought she could catch me out when my guard was down. Never.

'Don't even start, man. I was only talking to her.'

'Anyway, Mr Private Detective, time you got to bed.'

'I'm not a child, Mum,' I replied, watching Nanny, who had remained very quiet since we had returned. 'You all right, Nanny?' I asked him.

'Me cool, man. Just thinking 'bout things, y'know?'

'Yeah.' I looked at my mum again and saw how tired she looked. 'I think you're the one that needs to be in bed, Mum. You look really tired.'

My mum ruffled my hair and smiled. 'I always look tired, Sleepy. I'm old and wrinkly.'

116

'No you're not. You're quite fit for a dinosaur!'

Nanny burst out laughing.

'You can't talk to your *mother* like that, Sleepy,' Mum said, through a grin. 'Fit? What does that mean anyway?'

I began to speak but she cut me off.

'And as for you, Mr Dreadlocks Detective – less of your cheek too, unless you want to spend the rest of the night on the sofa.'

Nanny stopped laughing and started to mumble something under his breath about how I always got him into shit with my mum. I thought about replying, but then I remembered the song that Sally had been singing. I asked my mum if she had the CD it was on.

'UB40? Funny request from you. You're always telling me that they're old farts, Sleepy,' she said, smiling.

'No I'm not. I like them. I mean, how could I not like them? You've brought me up on their music. Man, it's all you listen to. Reggaemylitis you've got, Mum.'

It was true, too. Because of my mum being such a big fan I knew a lot of their music but had never really paid attention to the song that Sally had sung. I did quite like them too, only it was hard to admit that to my mates, who mostly thought they were too old and only listened to the latest trendy stuff, whatever it happened to be. But then again, I didn't know a single person who didn't know the words to at least one of their songs.

My mum went into the living room and came back with a CD. 'There you go, Sleepy.'

'*Geffrey Morgan?*' I said, more to myself than my mum, as I took the CD from her. I looked at the cover.

'The full title is *Geffrey Morgan Loves White Girls*,' she said, smiling.

I looked at her suspiciously. 'That's a mad name,' I said.

'Yeah and very apt for you too, don't you think, kid?'

I smiled. She was trying again. Man, when was she gonna learn? 'Oh stop it! Stop it! My sides are about to split. No more jokes, please!'

Later on, as I lay in bed listening to UB40, I thought about Sally and about the younger girl, Claire, who had run out of the house, wondering if either of them would get into trouble because they had helped us. I also wondered whether the Crew were going to get any more trouble over the money. After all, the man who had warned Jas had asked for it back – the second bag that we didn't have. I decided that I would have to ask Ellie about it in the morning – see if her kidnapper had mentioned anything about it. If she was up to it, of course.

I wanted to ask her about the kiss too but I decided not to. After all, it was just an emotional reaction to being rescued. Wasn't it? The song that Sally had been singing came on, 'The Pillow', and I shut my eyes and listened to the way the saxophone on it made the whole sound seem seedy and dirty; the way the vocalist sang from the point of view of a working girl. I thought about loads of stuff, random thoughts and not so random, and I didn't fall asleep until dawn.

nineteen:

thursday afternoon

The next day the Crew gathered round at Ellie's house. I got there before everyone else and brought Zeus with me, literally dragging him out of his basket and out of the door. He whinged and whined and dribbled until I got him into Ellie's house and then his whole demeanour changed when he saw her. He wagged his stump of a tail, stopped dribbling and, when Ellie petted him and called him 'stupid dog', he finally looked happy again.

'He's missed you,' I told her, smiling.

'Bloody thing. I haven't missed him,' she replied.

I knew she was lying. I looked into her eyes and saw that she still looked sad. 'Are you OK?'

'No, not really. I wanted to go for a walk but I can't. Not on my own.'

'I'll take you,' I offered, not getting it.

'Oh, you old man. It's not about the actual *going out* for a walk. It's the fact that I don't want to go on my *own*.'

I said sorry and this time got called a 'silly old man' for my trouble. 'Look, it's bound to be hard for you at first but you'll soon feel better,' I said.

'I know. The thing is – I'm still really scared and I don't want to be.' She started to cry.

'Hey, hey. Ellie, you're safe. We're all here to protect you.'

'I don't want to be protected. I want to feel normal – and I don't at the moment. What if I stay like this? You see stories about . . .'

I put my arms around her and smiled. 'You'll be fine, Baby. You're stronger than that. Come on, you've only just got home. In a few days you'll be moaning at me about being bored and how much you need to get blue trainers to match your latest blue top and all that.' I gave her a kiss on her forehead and she snuggled into my shoulder, still crying.

'I'm sorry,' she said. 'I'm being a silly little girl.'

I smiled at her again. 'But, Ellie, you *are* a silly little girl.'

That made her smile a little bit. She looked into my eyes. 'That's twice you've saved me now,' she said.

'Well, this time I had your dad and Nanny with me,' I said. '*And* I got a kiss for my trouble.' Instantly, I wished I hadn't said it.

'Yeah, I'm sorry about that,' replied Ellie, looking away.

'Hey, it's cool. You were glad to see me – I mean, all three of us.'

She looked at me again. Then she looked down. 'Let's forget about it. I feel silly for doing it.'

'Yeah,' I replied, wondering what the big deal was. 'It's forgotten, Baby.'

I'd just let her go when there was a knock on her bedroom door and Della walked in with Jas. Della screamed in delight when she saw Ellie and jumped on her, kissing her on the cheek over and over again.

'We ain't here for a show,' Jas said, smiling and ruffling Ellie's hair. 'Hey, kid.'

'You're just jealous because you can't do it,' laughed Della, making Jas turn the colour of beetroot

'Oh, get off me, you old woman!' Ellie complained, as Della continued to fuss over her.

'No way, sister. I'm going to be attached to you from now on. Like a rash, Baby!'

'Oh, that's sooo . . . nice,' replied Ellie, turning up her nose.

'I don't know,' I said, smiling. 'Della would make such a pretty rash too.'

'Oh stop it! You're both crazy,' Ellie laughed – her first laugh since before she had been kidnapped. It was amazing the effect that Della had on her. They messed around for a while longer, calling each other 'honey' and 'sexy' and then 'tart' and 'minx', before breaking down in hysterics over a joke that only they found funny. I think it was a girl thing.

Will turned up about half an hour after the other two and nearly got knocked over by Zeus as he entered the room. Zeus had caught the mood and was trying to join in with the hugging and joking and laughter, only his contribution was to jump at Will when the door opened, nearly giving him a cardiac. Will had to sit down on the bed to get over it and as soon as he sat down Della jumped on him too, kissing him on the forehead.

'Get off me, you fool!' Will pushed Della away but she just laughed.

'Ahh! Is poor Willy feelin' shy?'

'Shut up, you weirdo,' he said, wiping his forehead. 'You left spit all on me head. Nasty child.'

'Don't be upset, Daddy,' said Ellie jokingly. 'We're only playin' with you . . .'

At that both she and Della burst into more hysterics and Will just shut his eyes and groaned.

Zeus got involved again and jumped onto the bed, using Will as a stepping stone. After that it was chaos in there, as we told jokes, laughed, took the piss out of each other and generally celebrated the fact that we were all back together again.

After we had eaten an Indian takeaway that Jas and Della had gone to fetch, the rest of the Crew went home, leaving me and Ellie alone with Zeus. We talked a bit more about the kidnapping and Ellie told me about the girl, Claire, and how they had spoken about the kidnapper. Ellie described how scared the girl had looked and what the man's voice had sounded like. Then she told me that he had this really nasty, musty smell that followed him around.

'It's kind of like old socks,' she said, 'with a mask of aftershave. Like he doesn't wash but wears deodorant instead.'

'Sounds sexy,' I said, trying to make a joke out of it, but the thought of her kidnapper made Ellie shudder and at one point she started to cry again a little bit.

'I think it was the same man that was in the alley, Billy. The smell was the same.'

'The one you were telling us about . . . ?'

'I think so.'

My heart sank. If it really was the same man then we

weren't out of the woods yet. Not with the second bag still out there.

Ellie began to cry again. I let her this time, realizing that she needed to let it all out. I couldn't even imagine what it must have felt like for her, being held in that room with some nasty man threatening her, not knowing if he would harm her or not. I sat and listened to her as she spoke about what was going on in her head, then watched her fall asleep before leaving for mine, minus Zeus, who had fallen asleep on Ellie's bed with her.

I was smiling as I walked back into my mum's, realizing that Ellie would be well pissed off when she woke up in a pool of Zeus' saliva, his big, sweaty head resting next to her. Personally, I had barred him from my bed. I loved him and all that but there were limits, you know?

But eventually my mind was taken up with what Ellie had said. If it was the same man – the one from the alley – then we were going to hear a lot more about it. Guaranteed. You know when you hope that things are going to be fine, fully aware that it's just wishful thinking? Well, that's the thought that kept me awake until the break of dawn, as I turned things over and over in my mind . . .

I was right to be so concerned.

twenty:

a few days later ...

It took Ellie a few days to get back on her feet and feel able to go outside without getting scared. The first time Della and me went with her. She managed to walk around the block before deciding that it was a horrible day, which it was, and making for my bedroom, where the three of us sat and watched videos on my tiny television. Will was working with his dad during the day and Jas was continually at the gym, skateboarding or at kick boxing.

I had found a job recently, labouring on a building site, but I hadn't gone back after the first week. I mean, the money had been really good but I'd hated it. The other lads had all been loud-mouthed white blokes who'd thought it was clever to call me Gunga Din and tell me that I was all right for a Paki. After the first four times of telling, I'd had enough. I reckon I would have battered one of them if I had gone back. The trouble was that the agency that had found me the job had then been on my case, offering me two days at this factory and three days at that warehouse. In the end I'd rung them up and told them to get lost. Which they did.

Everything had settled down after Ellie's rescue and none of the Crew had run into Busta or any of his boys. It was only a matter of time before we did, however. There was no way that Busta would allow us to get away with hassling his gang and messing with his 'runnin's'. And there was still the question of the second bag and the people who had grabbed Jas. We had received no new warnings about it, but that was only because the police had been all over us since Ellie's return, interviewing and assessing and offering her and her family counselling. Victim support groups and that kind of stuff. Ellie had flat refused, though, and I didn't really blame her. She didn't need a shrink to tell her why she was feeling so low. It was obvious why. And with my mum and all of us to help her through, what she really needed was just time – any fool could have told her that. And more often than not, I did.

Life in the ghetto just carried on as normal. A mosque had been fire-bombed and a couple of asylum-seekers, Albanians, had been savagely beaten up the road from the community centre. The working girls were still out by the church and got younger every day, while the dealers and the pimps got fat and bought new drug-mobiles, covering them in stupid go-faster stripes, blacking out the windows and installing bass bins that shook my bedroom window as they passed. Things in paradise never changed.

There had also been a newspaper report about thefts from the police custody locker room at the Central Station. Nanny had alerted me to it, laughing about it at the kitchen table one evening, as Ellie and I sat and squabbled over which video to hire from the local shop.

Apparently 'someone' had stolen into the station late at night and taken drugs and cash. The 'someone' had then slipped out without any of the thirty coppers at the station noticing.

'Man, them mek me laugh till me cry,' said Nanny gleefully.

'How did they not see or hear anything being taken?' I wondered out loud.

Nanny just smirked. 'Because dem t'ief the drug themself, man.'

'You what?'

Nanny folded the newspaper and put it down on the table. 'Just las' week I man did talk to a friend of mine down by de churchyard an' him tell me that the Babylon a steal drug from de station and sell them back to the dealer.'

I was shocked. 'No way, man. That ain't never happening.'

'Yes, man. The same ting happen in London and Birmin'ham last year. Me read about it in a yuh mother's paper – is what you call it? De *Guardian*.'

'Well, how come I never saw that? I read the paper every day.'

Ellie yawned at us both and then smiled. 'Is Nanny talking that way deliberately – so I don't understand? Is it a boy thing?'

'Ellie,' I said, looking at her and shaking my head.

She grinned. 'Well – it's not very polite, is it?' Her grin got wider.

'Nanny, can you please talk normally – whatever *that* is – because Ellie would like to join in too and she can't . . .' I began.

'. . . understand you when you talk like Beenie Man,' finished Ellie.

'I'm sorry, darlin'. I was jus' telling Sleepy here about the way de police is selling confiscated drugs back to the dealers.'

Ellie's grin grew again. Pure Cheshire Cat wide. 'I know,' she said, getting up from the table. 'I just wanted to see if I could get you to speak differently.'

Nanny and me both looked at her and asked the same question. Why?

'Because I'm bored,' she replied.

And with that she left us there, mouths wide open, and went back next door.

Nanny smiled and shook his head. 'Billy, is one clever little gal yuh have there, y'know.'

'She isn't my "gal", man,' I protested, but Nanny just gave me a knowing look and then told me that it was time for him to get his 'spiritual meditation'.

He got up and tapped the paper as he left the table. 'Like Bob Marley sing, man. Read it in de news.'

Later on Della sent me a text, asking if she could come over for some curry. I sent her one back explaining that neither my mum nor Nanny had made any and, with Nanny out and my mum at an evening class, I was getting my own supper. She came round anyway and we shared a box of spicy chicken wings and chips that we got from a halal takeaway down at the end of my road. The wings were exactly what they were advertised as – HOT – and as we sat at the kitchen table talking, my mouth was burning. I was trying to listen to Della but all I could think about was how much water it would

127

take to make the tingling sensation in my mouth go away.

'. . . and he reckons I should go for it.'

'Sorry, Dell, I didn't hear you,' I said, getting myself a long glass of water.

'Which bit?'

'Er . . . all of it?'

Her eyes lit up. With anger. 'You what? You mean you ain't listened to a word of what I've been saying?'

'I couldn't. My mouth's burning, man. Tell me again.'

'No,' she replied, sulking. 'Anyway, I came round to talk about something else.'

'What's that then?'

'You gotta promise not to laugh at me though.'

I smiled at her.

'I mean it, Billy.'

'Yeah, OK. I promise.'

'Well, me and . . . er. Me and Jas – we've kind of got together, y'know?'

I did know. It would have taken a blind man not to see that there was something going on with those two. All those sly little looks between them. Laughing at each other's jokes. Always going everywhere together. Yeah, I'd noticed and so had Will and Ellie probably. I didn't let on to Della though.

'Really?' I said, trying and failing to sound surprised.

'Oh come on, Billy. I know that you know. Don't feign no surprise.' She looked me right in the eye.

'Well, it's not hard to see, Dell. I mean – all that whispering and giggling like kids and that.'

'Well, I thought I'd tell you anyway. Officially.'

'Cool,' I said, secretly quite pleased that they were going out. It had been on the cards for a while and they did suit each other.

'It's just that . . .' she said, before stopping.

I waited a few beats and then raised my eyebrows at her. 'Spit it out, Della. What else?'

'He won't . . . he doesn't want to . . .'

I sighed. 'What?'

'Well, we've been . . . erm . . . we've been intimate but not all the way.'

I looked away and then back at her. 'Hey, kid. More info than I need, y'know?'

'Billy, you said you wouldn't take the piss . . .' She wasn't angry though. More embarrassed than anything else.

'I'm sorry . . . go on, finish what you were saying.'

'He don't wanna sleep with me yet – least that's how it seems – and I don't know why. That's all.'

I put my stupid cap on. 'Have you asked him why?' I knew as soon as it left my mouth what her reaction would be.

'*Billy!*'

'Yeah, I know. Dumb. 'Course you've asked him.'

'He says that he's not ready yet, but I don't know. What if he doesn't fancy me?' She said it and immediately looked sad.

'Hey, he fancies the arse off you, kid. Come on, you know the way he looks at you. Maybe he ain't ready, like he says. Maybe he's scared.'

She flashed me a cold look. '*Scared? Of me?*'

'Not you, Della. Scared of the situation. You know, the whole thing about being friends and not wanting to mess that up. Or maybe he just wants to wait until it feels right. Or til you're sixteen. Out of respect, like.'

'Oh.'

I told her to talk to Jas. After all, it was his business, not mine, even though he had told me about it already. But Jas had made me promise not to tell Della and I wasn't about to break a confidence. Thing was, Jas hadn't ever had sex before – not all the way – which bothered him in case he messed up somehow. He was worried about them falling out too. Scared that it would put a huge dent in their friendship. But it was none of my business and I felt a bit embarrassed, to tell the truth. At the same time, I felt glad too. Happy that Della trusted me enough to tell me intimate stuff. I felt special.

When my mum returned, she took Della home. I told her that I'd call her the next day and left it at that. I didn't know then that the day after would bring what it did. How could I?

twenty-one:

tuesday,
11.15 a.m.

It started off like any other day. I got out of bed after eleven and sat in the living room drinking coffee and watching interior design programmes and talk shows featuring couples with major problems and no shame, all of which they wanted to share with the world. I was thinking about what I was going to do with my life. About how boring it was to have no job and no school to go to. I knew what I wanted to do – go to college and finish my education, be a journalist or something – but it seemed like a distant dream. I mean, who would take on the challenge of a young man with 'social problems' – as my last school principal had put it. Apparently I had no respect for the system, which was fine with me. The system didn't respect me either so the feeling was mutual. Reciprocal. I yawned through to just after midday and then had a shower before heading down to the kitchen to get some food. Nanny was at the table, looking at a vegetarian cook book and listening to a Bob Marley CD.

'What you gonna make for us today, Ainsley?'

I began pottering in the cupboards and the fridge,

trying to find something appealing to eat. Nanny didn't even look up at me but grinned anyway.

'I don't know, man. I was thinking about aloo gobi but we nuh have any potatoes in de house. I might go to the market.'

'Cool.' There was nothing that I wanted so I settled for sawdust, which is what I called muesli.

'Unless you want go for me?' said Nanny, closing the book and looking up. 'You know – justify your existence for today instead of mooching 'round da house.' His dreads were tied back on his head today and his beard was beginning to show flecks of grey. Salt and pepper dread.

'I could – I wasn't planning on going up town but I might. Let me see what Dell and Ellie are doing later.'

'Ellie pass by this morning. She say that she was going shopping with her muddah.'

'What time, Nan?' It was a silly question. She would have been really early – by my clock anyway.

''Bout ten. Tol' me to call you lazy bwoi.'

'Listen – a man needs his sleep, y'know.'

I couldn't understand how people got out of bed so early, even on days when they had nothing to do. Ellie never slept in. In fact she was always banging on at me about how I missed the better part of the day by sleeping in like I did. I told her that I was a night person once and she went out and bought me some vampire fangs from a joke shop. And some garlic for herself. Strange child.

'Sleep is an escape for fools, Billy. Yuh get nuff time fe sleep when yuh dead.' Nanny was at it again, the dread philosopher, quoting Bob Marley, I think.

'Well, then I'm a fool, man,' I replied, sitting at the table with my bowl of wood chippings, dried mouse droppings and plastic strawberries.

I walked into the city centre later that afternoon, past the high-rise blocks and over the railway bridge, via the concrete carriageway that separated the ghetto from the city. I didn't actually have anything to do in town other than buy some vegetables for Nanny but I rarely *did* have anything to do. That was one of the problems with not knowing what you wanted to do with your life. I didn't have a clue. Going back to school or college crossed my mind again but the thought had the lifespan of a butterfly. Town was like a little escape from boredom and a chance to meet up with a few people I knew. I spent most of the afternoon in and out of HMV and Virgin, looking at CDs that I couldn't really afford, or window shopping for trainers.

I went into the market and found the veg stall that Nanny always went to. It was run by an old Trinidadian couple and they knew me well. I picked up a few bits and handed them to Mr Dennis, the stall holder.

'A' right, Billy. How yuh doin'?'

'Cool, Mr Dennis. Just shopping for Nanny.'

Mr Dennis asked after Nanny and then my mum. Finally he stuffed everything I had picked up into a green carrier bag and gave it to me. 'Me t'row in some real hot pepper, too. No charge. Jus' tell Nanny to keep shy of usin' too much of dem, yuh hear?'

I grinned. 'Why, are they mega hot then?'

'Bwoi, dem is real life Scotch Bonnet – original hot stepper pepper. No substitute, man.'

'Wicked,' I replied, hoping that Nanny would use a few later.

'Tek it easy, Billy.'

'You too, Mr Dennis. And give my love to your wife.'

As I walked away, Mr Dennis had already moved into a new conversation with his next customer, telling him about the best way to fry plantain. I walked through a W.H. Smith, which linked the market square with one of the main shopping streets in the city, ignoring the security guard who told me I couldn't use the store as a pathway. Out on the street gangs of kids milled around, getting in the way and on the nerves of the older shoppers. Some of them did this on purpose, trying to get a rise out of some poor shopper, who would react and then get a barrage of obscenities for his or her trouble. In some cases they might even be physically assaulted. I'd seen it happen. I walked calmly past all the gangs, wearing my 'don't mess' mask that everyone in my area developed after a while.

Back in my own neighbourhood I let my 'screwface' relax and I sauntered home. I walked down the side street that led to the alley, first dodging a mad ginger tom cat that ran out from behind a pile of old newspapers and cardboard boxes, then noticing a piece of tin foil on the ground by the boxes. I realized that if I had the energy or the inclination to look further, I'd find a hypo and a spoon too, but I didn't bother. Heroin paraphernalia wasn't on my shopping list. I walked down the alley, into the constant gloom that darkened the alley year round, regardless of the time of day. There were three large bins just to the right of my back door and as I approached them I heard the soft sound of moaning coming from behind them. I assumed it would be a wino or maybe the junkie who had left the evidence in the alleyway entrance. Not bothering to look, I opened the door to the yard and walked through. Behind me the moaning got louder. Whoever was by the bins was trying to say something. I turned to close the door and a figure stood up in the gloom – a female figure in a blue, denim skirt and a torn, baby blue top. Blood ran from a gash above her eyes and her blonde hair was matted and stuck to her head. I looked again. Her blue trainers were covered in mud and her legs were bruised. Her top was torn open and her bra ripped. There were dark marks on her breasts and her neck. I dropped the bag I was carrying as she reached out for my arm.

'. . . B–B–Billy . . .'

I started to shake as her face came out of the gloom. 'Oh shit!'

twenty-two:

tuesday, 5 p.m.

'Where is she?'

My mum had raced back from work straight after I'd called her. She looked flustered and worried. After cleaning the gash on Sally's forehead and lending her a pair of my jeans and a top to change into, I'd shown her where my bedroom was and left her there. As soon as her head had hit the pillow she'd passed out. I hadn't known whether to call an ambulance or the police or what, but I was sure that Sally would prefer to see my mum. Taking off her coat in the kitchen, my mum was trying to get everything straight before going up to her.

'Where did you find her?' she asked, pacing around the kitchen like an upset teacher.

'She was in the alley when I got back from town,' I told her.

'Has she told you who hurt her?'

'No, Mum, she hasn't. All she keeps banging on about is some girl.'

'Who?'

'I don't know. I can't really understand her.'

'And you think she's had drugs?'

'Yeah, I think so. She was all drowsy and not just from the cut on her head. Her pupils are like pinpricks and—'

My mum cut me off. 'Let me go and check on her.'

'Mum, be careful. She's been beaten up.'

She came over and gave me a quick hug. 'It's all right, Billy. I know how to handle it. It's what I do every day.' She let go of me and walked out of the kitchen, telling me to make her a cup of coffee.

My mum was up in my room with Sally for about an hour and her coffee had gone cold by the time she came back downstairs. I put the kettle on again and started to make her a fresh coffee.

'Turn that off, Billy. I don't want one.' She looked careworn.

I wanted to go over and give her a hug but I didn't know whether I could. She looked really upset, sad almost, with a faraway look in her eyes and on her face. I made myself another cup of coffee instead and went over to the table with it.

'She won't tell me what happened.' Mum cleared her throat before continuing, 'Or should I say, who did that to her. I can see what happened.'

'She's been beaten up real bad, hasn't she?' It was yet another one of my stupid comments. I was like a Ninja black belt at stating the obvious.

'Billy, she's been tortured. She's got cigarette burns on her chest and neck.'

'Oh shit . . .' I had to gulp down anger and tears and—

'She needs to see a doctor but she won't let me call an ambulance.'

'Why not? Surely if she's that badly hurt, she needs to go to hos—'

'She's scared, Billy. Really scared. She keeps on talking about her friend Claire.'

Claire – the young girl who had been left in the empty house with Ellie. The one who had helped her escape by telling Sally where she was. The one who had run past me as I entered the house the night we found Ellie.

'Listen, do you want me to go talk to her?'

'Not right now, Billy. She's out of it. She's had a lot of heroin by the look of it.'

I shook my head.

'Right, let me think. I can't call the police. I can't call an ambulance because they'll report her injuries to the police. What am I gonna do?'

She sat and went over the options again and again. Not that there was a lot to think over. We *had* to call an ambulance. That was the only sensible thing to do. I pointed out that we didn't have to tell anyone that we had spoken to Sally and I knew that she wouldn't tell the police anything. It wasn't like we were betraying her trust, was it? We were doing the only thing we could do. I mean, it wasn't like a crime novel where the characters always seemed to know dodgy back-street doctors who would remove a bullet for a small fee and all that. It just didn't happen in real life – well not in mine anyway.

'Right, that's settled. Billy, call an ambulance and I'll go and check on Sally.'

'OK. Where shall I tell them we found her?'

'Just say the alleyway. Tell them that you know her because she's local and that you found her exactly the way that you did. Just don't tell them that she's been here for a while.'

'Right.'

The ambulance took less than twenty minutes to arrive at the house and it was followed a few moments later by a police car. Five minutes after that, two CID officers turned up in an unmarked police car. The uniformed officers spoke to the ambulance crew and then to me while my mum spoke to one of the CID officers. It was DI Lucy Elliot – the one who had turned up when we'd rescued Ellie and I could tell she was incredibly suspicious of what my mum was telling her, even when she gave her the clothes Sally had been wearing – 'evidence', I guess. The ambulance crew brought Sally downstairs and put her on a gurney with wheels. Sally didn't really know what was going on. She was sobbing and moaning about Claire as the crew took her out to the ambulance. A crowd had gathered in the road and two local kids were sitting in the marked police car, messing with the radio. As the ambulance door closed, one of the kids managed to find the siren switch and it went off. One of the uniforms swore and ran over to the car, only for the youths to jump out, calling him 'bacon bwoi', and run off up the road and away. The copper didn't bother to chase them. I think he was used to it. He merely switched the siren off and returned to the house after locking the car.

'Bloody kids,' he muttered as he passed me and my mum.

Behind us, DI Elliot was standing looking at her notebook. She flipped it shut and came up to us. 'Are either of you going to the hospital with her?'

'No, not yet,' replied my mum. 'I might go up later.'

'Right, can we talk?' asked DI Elliot. She nodded at the house. 'Inside.'

We turned and headed into the house, just as the two uniformed officers came back out with the second CID and headed for the alley entrance. The crowd was still there. Young kids were pointing and throwing mumbled insults at the police. A couple of old women stood gossiping and shaking their heads in disgust. Next to the police car another youth lounged, sniggering through his gold-toothed mouth. 'YOW! BABYLON!' he shouted at the two uniforms.

They looked up and saw the kid by their car. Somehow he had forced the window down despite the car being locked. One of the coppers unclipped his handcuffs and ran over to the car but the kid had gone by the time he got there, disappearing down the road after his mates in a flash of Nike trainers and Adidas tracksuits. The shouts from the crowd echoed as the copper pulled strips of streaky bacon from his dashboard. Judging by the state of the youths who had left the meat, it was definitely smoked.

twenty-three:

tuesday, 7 p.m.

'Your story doesn't seem to add up.' DI Elliot was sitting facing me and my mum at our kitchen table, her notebook open.

My mum looked at me and then turned to Elliot. 'What's to add up?' she said, leaning forward in her chair. 'It's what happened.'

DI Elliot softened her gaze and tried to look concerned. 'I appreciate that it's been a difficult time for you both. First your friend goes missing and then this happens.'

This time I shrugged. 'What has *that* got to do with this?' I asked her, looking at her directly.

'Well, it's a bit of a coincidence, isn't it? I mean, why did the girl . . .' She looked at her notes. 'Why did Sally turn up at your house when you only know her from around the area?'

'Dunno.'

'Doesn't that seem strange to you? A girl who has been badly beaten doesn't go the police, doesn't get herself to hospital – she comes here instead.' Elliot returned my stare.

'Maybe she was beaten up in the alleyway,' suggested my mum. 'She was hardly in a state to get to the hospital by herself.'

'We must have been the closest place for her to get to,' I added, supporting my mum.

'Possibly,' answered Elliot. She didn't look convinced but then she didn't know any more about what had happened than we did. Glancing at her notes once more, she continued, 'So you do know who she is but you don't *actually* know her – as in, you aren't friends or anything?'

'No,' I replied.

'But you do know that she's a sex-worker?'

My mum spoke up. 'Yes, we do. What difference does that make?'

'I'm wondering whether you've seen her with a boyfriend maybe? Or a pimp?'

'No – no we haven't,' replied my mum, frowning. The little creases on her forehead and by the sides of her eyes took on life.

'How about you, Billy?' asked Elliot. 'Do you know where she lives, or any of her friends?'

I waited for a moment before replying, not wanting to tell her anything more than I had to. 'I've seen her around, said hello and that. But I've never seen her with a pimp or anything.' I hesitated, then added, worried about Josh. 'I think she's got a kid, but his granny looks after him or something like that. But I don't know where she lives, or anything.'

'How about the other girl? Claire? Do you know her?'

I looked at my mum for a split second and then back at Elliot. 'No, I don't know her.'

Elliot eyed me with suspicion. 'Are you sure, Billy? It's very important.'

'Yes, I'm sure.'

DI Elliot flipped her notebook shut and put it down on the table. She must have been between thirty and thirty-five years of age and she was quite attractive. She also seemed different to most of the other coppers I had met in my life. For one thing, she was female and not in a uniform. I wondered whether she was part of the new breed of recruits that were used in adverts to encourage applications from women and from ethnic minorities. Part of the 'changing face of policing' that I had read about in the papers. Her hair was short and blonde and her eyes were the same colour as mine, almost amber. She was a little taller than me and, if she wasn't in the police force, I would have said she was quite fit for an older women. But she was a copper. Part of 'Babylon army', as Nanny would put it.

Realizing that I was giving her the once-over, she looked away briefly before leaning forward on the table, hands clasped. 'I know that people round here distrust the police for a number of reasons,' she said, looking directly at me.

I shrugged.

'I even understand it, up to a point.'

I looked at my mum and frowned too. I could feel it coming – the speech about rotten apples and shit – but DI Elliot surprised me.

'The force *has* got racist officers. Sexist too. There *is* corruption.'

'You can say that again. Most of the coppers round here treat us like animals in a zoo,' I told her.

'I understand that,' she continued. 'But some of us, the vast majority, are here to help people. To stop crime. That's what we get paid to do.'

'So, why don't you do it?' I asked. 'Why are you always out chasing kids dealing in weed and persecuting the working girls and that?'

'Let me—' she began.

I cut her off. She wasn't getting out of this one. 'No, just answer the question, man. I've seen the police cars driving around, right past the crack dealers and the heroin pushers. Hassling the youth and leaving the big-time people alone.'

'We're trying, Billy. But we can't get anywhere if the locals treat us like stormtroopers.' She looked at my mum, who just sat and frowned.

'Who the cap fit, man,' I replied. Let them wear it.

She ignored me. 'This incident with Sally – someone around here will know what happened but no one will ever talk to us. I mean, we still don't even know who made the call to tell you where Ellie Sykes was being held.'

I had to give her credit – it was a sly move. Trying to catch me with my guard down. 'We told you,' I said. 'It was an anonymous call. Some girl—'

'And you've had no other calls? Or threats?'

'No. But you know that because you've spoken to Ellie.'

'Yes – she told us that her kidnappers had a young girl keep an eye on her. But she didn't give us the girl's name.'

'I suppose she didn't know it,' I replied, looking at my mum.

'And within a few days a young girl, badly assaulted, turns up on your doorstep, drugged to the eyeballs and mumbling about someone called Claire. I can't help thinking that there is a link.'

'So what *is* the link?' I asked, standing up.

'I don't know,' confessed Elliot. 'I'm still trying to find it.'

'If there actually is one,' added my mum, finally getting involved.

Elliot looked over at her.

'Please don't think I'm being rude,' continued my mum, 'but this isn't getting us anywhere. I don't understand what you are asking my son.'

'I'm trying to ascertain what actually occurred.'

'And we've told you: we've given statements to your colleagues and answered your questions with patience. But, as I said, to no apparent avail, so if you've finished – I wouldn't mind getting on with the rest of my day.'

Elliot stood up and pocketed her notebook. 'You're right, Mrs—' She stopped when she realized her mistake but didn't rectify it. Instead she pulled out a card and put it on the table. 'If you remember anything or have anything further to add, my number's on the card. It's direct and it's totally confidential.' She was looking straight at me. I looked away.

My mum stood up and opened the kitchen door for Elliot, shaking her hand out of politeness.

'Thank you for talking to me. I'll have to arrange a time to go over your statements properly – at your convenience,' said Elliot, walking towards the kitchen door. 'I can see myself out.'

twenty-four:

tuesday, 8 p.m.

The Crew came round an hour later and we sat in my bedroom, talking things over. I had been thinking, fretting, continuously since DI Elliot had left.

The facts were pretty clear. We'd found a bag full of money which we had then handed in to the coppers. *Someone* had watched us. That *someone* knew that we had been to the police. That same person *might* have put a brick through my mum's window – maybe as a warning. After that Ellie, who had complained about seeing a strange man a few times, had been kidnapped. Sally had told us where Ellie was being held after getting a message from the younger girl, her friend Claire. While Ellie was being held we had got a warning about a second bag – the night that Jas was threatened – and then we had found Ellie. Since that night all had been quiet until I had found Sally, badly beaten up. What if she was a message, saying, 'Hand over the second bag – or else'?

Della and Jas were sitting together on my bed when Will arrived with Ellie. Jas was trying not to make it too obvious that he and Della were seeing each other, even

146

though we all knew. I think he was still feeling a bit embarrassed by it all.

Will grinned at them as soon as he walked in. 'Ah, the happy couple.'

'Hush your mouth, Willy,' replied Della jokingly. 'There's a good little lamb.'

Will smirked at her and then plonked himself down next to the both of them, leaving me standing with Ellie, worrying about the maximum strain that could be placed on my bed without it falling apart.

Ellie started things rolling. 'Why are we all here then?' she asked, looking at me.

'We need to have a conference,' I said. 'Things have been happening and I think we're about to get some more trouble.'

Jas perked up at the mention of trouble. 'Yeah? Who is it this time – not that wanker Busta again?'

I shook my head. 'No – at least, I don't think it's him.'

I pulled out the card that DI Elliot had left for me and twirled it between my fingers and thumb. I wondered where to begin my story and decided to start at the beginning.

'I found that working girl today – Sally. She was out round the back of the houses.'

'I heard about something goin' on earlier,' said Will. 'One of the lads up the road from me said that they'd found a junkie – I didn't think anything of it though.'

'They found *Sally*,' I replied.

Ellie's eyes grew wide with a mixture of what seemed like fear and surprise. 'Wh-what was up with her?'

'She was beaten up, Ellie.'

'How do you mean?' asked Della, sitting up straight.

I had their full attention now. I told them about the rest of it – the police and the questions from DI Elliot and all that. They listened in silence, which was a first for one of our gatherings. Man, keeping Della and Will quiet for longer than five minutes was a first – full stop.

'So that copper, Idiot or whatever – she thinks that we know more than we're sayin'?' asked Jas when I had finished.

'Her name's Elliot, Jas, and yeah, she's well sus' about the whole thing, man.'

'This is starting to feel a bit like a dodgy film plot,' added Della.

'No, little girl,' replied Will, 'this is real.'

'Who you callin' little girl?' Della flashed him a look that said, Shut up or else. Will just laughed.

'I don't see what's so funny,' I said, wondering whether I was the only one of us who thought things were getting a little bit serious.

'I'm scared,' Ellie said, looking at me. 'Sally was dumped in *our* alley. What if she was a warning . . . ?'

'It's all right, Ellie. Nothing else is gonna happen to you. I promise.' I was trying to be reassuring but my words came out as bravado and did nothing to calm Ellie's fears.

'What if they come after me again? What if they hurt one of us – seriously this time? Like they have with Sally.'

'They won't,' I said calmly. 'They'd have to be stupid to come after you again. The police would be all over them in a flash.'

'How, Billy? How would they? The police don't even know most of what's happened because we haven't told them,' argued Ellie.

Della sat back down on the bed. 'Well maybe it's time we did tell the police,' she said quietly.

'Tell them what?' interrupted Jas. 'That we all lied to them – even Ellie's dad, though he didn't know it?' He hammered home his point. 'Man, we go to them now and they are gonna take us in – including Ellie's old man.'

'So what do you suggest, Mr Detective? We go after them ourselves?' said Will, earning a glare from Jas for his trouble.

'And who exactly do we go after? We don't even know who they are?'

'Has this girl, Sally, told you who attacked her?' asked Della.

'No – she was completely out of it. In a real state. All she came out with was one name – Claire – the girl—' I began.

'— who they had watching me?' added Ellie, finishing my sentence for me with a question.

I looked at them both in turn. 'Yeah. Kept saying that they've got her.'

'But not who "they" actually are?' Della was thinking along the same lines as me. Know thy enemy.

'You want me to ask her, don't you?' I said. 'When she's recovered enough to talk.'

'Makes sense. Either that or get her to tell the police,' she replied.

'She won't talk to the police,' I told her. 'No way.'

'Then she has to tell you, Billy. It's the only way we'll know who is doing all of this. And then we can do something about it.'

'Which is *what* exactly?' asked Will, just beating Ellie and Jas to the same question.

Della looked at him and shrugged. 'I dunno,' she admitted.

'It's better to know who we are up against than not, though,' I said, supporting Della.

'In that case, you had better go and talk to her,' said Will.

'Oh, this is getting stupid,' moaned Ellie. 'We aren't the police. One of us will end up getting hurt. Can't we just hand it all over to them?'

I twirled the card DI Elliot had given me, getting an idea. 'Yeah, Ellie . . . we can. Let's just find out who we are dealing with first and then I'll give DI Elliot a call.'

'Nah, dread,' countered Jas. 'We's comin' like grasses, man.'

'Yeah, but we ain't stupid,' replied Della, shutting Jas up quick time.

'Honour amongst thieves and all that? You're living in cloud cuckoo land, Jas.' Will backed Della. 'Besides – whoever kidnapped Ellie is an effin' nonce,' he continued. 'It's our duty to grass up a nonce, man. Them nuh matter.'

'And from when they kidnap my sister here, then they got to pay.'

Della's eyes flashed with a look that I had only ever seen when she was really angry. It was a warning, a sign. It said, I'm not joking. It said we had better believe it, too.

twenty-five:
Wednesday afternoon

The ward where they were keeping Sally was full to breaking point with patients. The staff that were around looked tired and pissed off – as much in need of medical attention as the people they were looking after. The ward Sally was in was in a Victorian building that was part of the old hospital. All around it new buildings towered into the sky, blocking the sunlight and causing a deep gloom to cover the building I was standing in. The place smelt of age and death and disinfectant. The staircases were built of stone and looked as though they had been removed from a country manor and brought to the hospital, the banisters painted in a dirty dark green colour to add to the general air of depression. I hated hospitals anyway, but this one took the biscuit as far as doom and gloom were concerned.

Sally was dozing in her bed, a drip feeding its way through her hand and into her bloodstream. There were dark bruises on her face and neck and her bare arms showed signs of heroin use. She looked fragile, as if she would break if she tried to sit up or get out of bed. I had told the nurse at the desk that I was her boyfriend when she challenged me. She had given me a look that sat somewhere between contempt and pity, pointing to the end of the ward and not showing me to where Sally was. As I approached her bed, I'd felt like a real scumbag, eyes taking in my appearance and silent whispers behind my back from the other patients and their visitors. Did they think I'd been responsible for her injuries? But I had no time for feeling self-conscious. I had to talk to her. I had to find out who had hurt her.

She'd opened her eyes when I'd first approached, taking me in and then closing them again. Now she began to stir again and her eyes flickered open and shut, like they do when you're in a deep sleep and it gets interrupted. I pulled a chair up to the bed and sat down, leaning in. The smell of disinfectant and body odour mingled as I got closer to her and a tear worked its way down her cheek. She turned her head towards me, opening her eyes as wide as she could manage, smiling a bit, then coughing. I moved back through instinct and then, realizing what I had done, I leaned forward and stroked her forehead. It seemed the right thing to do somehow.

'Hi . . .' Her voice was like a croak, as if her mouth contained no moisture whatsoever.

'Hey, kid, how you doing?' Another stupid question.

She shifted in the bed and then opened her eyes fully, smiling a little more.

'I'm . . . well, you can see for yourself,' she said, after clearing her throat.

'I know. What have the doctors told you?'

She tried to laugh, but not in jest. It was a rueful laugh. 'They want me to talk . . . the police. I can't . . .'

'They can wait until you're ready.'

'No, Billy . . . I just can't tell . . . anything.'

I picked up a plastic beaker of water from a side cupboard by the bed and, tilting her head slightly, helped her to drink some.

'You don't have to tell them anything,' I told her, putting the beaker back in its place.

'I can't . . . even if I . . .'

'Why, Sally? Who did this?'

A look of terror overtook her. 'One of them . . . one of . . .'

'Who? A gang? Someone you know?' I didn't want to push her too hard but I had to find out. For everyone.

'No, Billy . . . one of them . . .' She looked away.

'Them *who*, Sally?' I asked, looking at her arms and seeing bruising of recent needle-tracks.

'. . . can't . . . sleep.'

She dozed off for about half an hour as I sat with her, thinking about what she had meant by 'them'. After about fifteen minutes a nurse walked up and checked Sally's charts and the drip by her bed. The nurse was young, African I think, and she smiled at me and then looked at Sally.

'Your friend – she is lucky,' the nurse told me, smiling broadly.

'I know,' I replied, looking away.

The nurse walked away and left me sitting there, wondering what was so lucky about having to sell your body to make money and being tortured by someone. Of course the nurse had meant that Sally was still alive and for that small mercy, we should be grateful. I thought back to some of the stuff that Nanny had told me about, the things he believed in. I didn't really believe in God as such, but I would have given thanks and praise to Jah if he'd only make it all better and sort the mess we were in. I suppose that made me a bit of a hypocrite.

I thought some more and then Sally came round again, asking me for some more water. I helped her to swallow a few mouthfuls and then she lay back again. I put the water back. She turned her head towards me.

'. . . put drugs in me,' she said, in a whisper.

'Who?' I asked, moving my head closer to her.

'They . . . injected me with . . . brown.' She had started to cry. I grabbed a tissue from a box next to the water and dabbed her face with it.

'I . . . I . . . off it . . . been th–three months. They made me . . .'

I found it hard to hear what she was saying at first but as she drank more water, her voice became stronger and after a while what she was saying became clearer and clearer. She had kicked her addiction to heroin three months ago, she told me, with the help of her son's grand-mother. She said that she had felt proud of herself and had decided to get a proper job and stop working out by the church, only her attackers had ruined it all. They had beaten her up and injected her with heroin. I don't know why she chose to tell me everything they had done to her, but she did, and I was in tears by the end, horrified at what human beings can do to each other. It made me angry and sad at the same time. How could they have done that to her? She was only a young girl. *A girl*.

I sat and listened to her for an hour and in that time she told me, again and again, what they had done but not who *they* were. I told her that she had to tell the police what she had been put through, if only to stop them from doing it to someone else. That was when she told me I was too late. That they had Claire. That Claire was dead. I asked her, over and over, who she was talking about. Who had hurt her and Claire? And then she told me, through tears and saliva, asking me to promise not to tell a soul. I really wanted to promise but I couldn't.

Not once she'd told me who they were.

I let her cry herself to sleep and then ran out of the hospital, lighting a fag as soon as I hit the street, my head spinning. I pulled out the card that DI Elliot had given me and looked at it before making a decision, pulling out my phone and dialling a different number . . .

twenty-six:

Wednesday, 4.00 p.m.

'So, have you and Jas – you know . . . ?'
I was in my bedroom with Della, trying to get her to tell me all about Jas. I wanted to know everything – every last detail – but Della wasn't playing. She was being all serious and womanly and adult. Boring.

'Please tell me . . .' I pleaded, sticking out my lower lip so that she'd feel sorry for me and tell me everything. And do you know what she did? She laughed at me and told me to try harder, just like Billy always did.

'You ain't catching me out, little monkey. That only works with Billy and that's only cause he fancies you,' she told me, smirking.

I pouted. 'No he doesn't . . . does he?'

'Ellie! Don't play with me, man. I'm your sister.'

'What?' I said, trying to hide the smile that was making its way across my face.

'See, you is even smilin' – what's up wid that?'

'Nothing, Della. Honest. And anyway – when did you become an American? Talking like that. Is it any wonder that I never understand a word you say?'

'Ellie . . .'

156

'Oh, all right. So I like to gossip. Please tell me, Della. Please . . .'

'Only if you admit that you know Billy likes you.'

I thought about it and smiled. Of course I knew Billy liked me. I liked him. But it wasn't like it was a big deal or anything. I mean, we didn't make it an issue. We didn't have to. Everyone else did that for us. My mum, my dad, Chris De Burgh. The rest of the Crew, Billy's mum and especially Della. She was always making little comments about it . . . drove Billy mad. Silly old man.

'Yeah, OK. But you can't tell him or I won't stop sulking for a year, all right?'

'Deal.'

Got her.

'Jas and me, we ain't actually done anything … well not that, anyway.'

I was on cloud nine. Major gossip alert.

'He keeps telling me that he's not ready yet. Says it's a big step and we should wait.'

I grinned at her. 'And you don't want to?' I asked.

'Sack that, man. 'Course I wanna. But only if it feels right y'know?'

I was still curious. 'So what have you been doing then?' I was hoping that she would tell me it all now that I had her guard down but she just went back to being an old woman.

'That's enough for now, young lady. You ain't old enough.'

'Don't be like that, Della. And I'm not that much younger than you. Legally, you're not old enough either.'

She just looked at me like I was a child. I was about to have a paddy. 'Your mum will kill me, Ellie. I can't corrupt you . . .' Now she was taking the piss out of me.

'Oh – old woman! I'm not going to tell my mum.'

'Well, let's just say, and this is between sisters, you understand, let's just say that him have all de machinery an' ev'ry piece
a work, man!'

We both started laughing. I was shocked. Della and Jas were
. . . well, you know, and she was telling me! Result or what?

'Tell me more, Dell. Please . . .'

'No, that's enough for now. But I'll do you a deal, Ellie . . .'

That wasn't part of the plan.

'I'll give you the details as and when things, y'know, happen,
and you can make me a cup of tea.'

'What – now?' Cheeky old woman!

'Yeah, come on – I'm parched.'

We were in the living room watching telly and drinking the tea
that I had persuaded my mum to make for us when my brother
walked in, whistling Lady in Red as usual. It was beginning to
get boring, but I let it go for once. Christopher came and sat down
next to me and Della and asked us what we'd been talking about
in my room.

'I heard you laughing. Like those witches in Macbeth.'

'Christopher! Don't call Della a witch. How rude is that?'

'Well? What were you on about?'

'Nothing for your young ears, my boy,' answered Della.
Christopher began to speak but Della held up her hand. 'Call me
a witch again and I'm gonna kick yo' ass, honey.'

He smiled at her. A wide, annoying I-don't-care kind of smile.
'You won't ever catch me, you old woman!'

'CHRIS DE BURGH!' I shouted, as he ran off out of the room,
chuckling to himself.

'Little bugger,' laughed Della as the local news started on the
telly. The first headline made us both stop in our tracks and stare
at the screen.

158

'. . . found beaten to death in an alley. The young girl, whose real name we cannot disclose due to her age, was a local prostitute known only as Claire . . .'

I looked at Della and started to shake. She sat wide-eyed, listening to the rest of the report.

'. . . Detective Inspector Elliot would like to hear from anyone who was in the vicinity of the community centre around the time of the discovery and also from anyone who may have known the victim. Any information will be treated in the strictest confidence. The number to call if you have information is . . .'

Della looked at me and then, seeing that I was shaking, took hold of my hand. 'It's OK, Ellie. You're safe, Baby.'

'It's her . . . it must be . . . the girl from the house . . .'

I tried to calm down, to think rationally, only it wouldn't happen. Didn't work. All those feelings of being scared came flooding back into my head and I wanted my dad.

'Ellie, stay here. I'm going next door. I'm gonna find Billy and the others. We've got to go to the police . . .'

twenty-seven:

wednesday, 5 p.m.

Nanny was in the kitchen doing his house-husband routine when I got back from the hospital. A reggae tape was playing as Nanny stirred some onions, beginning to make a curry. Culture – singing about Marcus Garvey and two sevens clashing or something. The smell took over the entire kitchen and reminded me of being a little kid – watching Nanny in our old flat as the telly flickered away, on but unwatched, and I asked him again and again where my mummy was. Then, as now, Nanny waited until he was ready before he spoke to me, despite what I had told him over the phone. He waited until the onions had softened, then added some finely chopped garlic and ginger before pouring in a touch of diluted tomato purée and starting on the masala. As the spices sizzled and popped, he raised the pan and twirled it in slow, flat half circles, making sure that the garam masala, turmeric and red chilli powder didn't stick to the bottom. Then, as I started to grow impatient, he added the purée mixture and set the pan back on the heat, turning the flame up until it reached boiling point before lowering the temperature, stirring the sauce and finally joining me at the table.

He sighed as he sat down, scratching his beard just under his chin. He waited for a moment longer and then asked me to tell him everything – in detail.

'I spoke to Sally,' I told him.

'She tell yuh who hurt her?'

'Yeah. It was Busta.'

He shook his head slowly and scratched his beard again. 'Why?' he asked, looking right into my eyes.

'It's a long, long story, Nan,' I replied, trying to get all the bits straight in my head.

'Tell me nuh, man. I have all de time yuh need.' He sat back in his chair.

'OK.'

I told him everything, exactly as Sally had told it to me, and all the way through he sat and listened intently, shaking his head now and then and playing with his facial hair. At one point he held up his hand to stop me, ran his hands over his dreads and then motioned for me to carry on. At the end he sat for a while, thinking about what I had said and then he asked me some questions.

'So the alley was bein' used as a drop and pick-up point for drugs and money?'

'Yeah, the man that Ellie kept seeing is some out-of-town contact that Busta was using.'

'Why use a man from out a town?'

'Busta thinks that the police have his whole crew under surveillance – that's why. No-one knows this guy so they just ignore him. Well the police, anyways.' I cleared my throat. 'There was only ever one bag of money. It was all a scam.'

'One? So why de raas is dat bwoi chattin' 'bout a secon' bag?'

'He's playin' out his scam, Nanny,' I explained. 'Busta told his boss that *two* bags went missing – thirty grand in all. When we handed in the bag with fifteen grand, Busta's boss knew what we had done. Maybe he's got someone working for him down at the police station – I dunno – but he knew. He must have called Busta straight away.'

'Seen,' Nanny said. 'Busta a tief fifteen grand and blame yuh crew.'

'Exactly.'

I continued my story, trying to get everything clear in my head. 'When the pick-up man told Busta the bag he'd left wasn't there, Busta was mad, but figured he could make a raise out of it by claiming he'd left two bags. That way he got to pocket fifteen grand. Then we gave the money to the coppers. When we handed that bag in we alerted his boss, who knew exactly how much money had been handed in – not the amount Busta said had gone missing – so Busta was stuck. He had to explain where all the money was and he blamed us. Said we had kept one bag. That's why he suddenly sent someone to put the brick through the window. He had to convince his boss that we were the thieves.'

'OK, dat part me understand. But how Busta know all a dis so quick? From when we hand in bag to when we get home? How him know so fast? Him some kind a obeah man?'

I raised my eyebrow. 'A *what-a-man*?'

'*Obeah*. It mean witch doctor man. Him psychic?'

'Dunno. But his boss must have a contact at the station. Sally told me that Busta works for a real connected man. No one knows who he is but he's using

Busta to sell drugs out on the street. You know all that cheap-grade brown that killed them junkies a few months back? That's all from Busta's boss. Sally said that this man is trying to corner the area all for himself. And he's got the power to do it.'

Nanny nodded sagely.

'Anyway it was Busta's boss who suggested the kid-napping. The guy that was doing the pick-ups is some old pervert and Busta got him to do it. That way, we were bound to give the second bag back. Or so Busta's boss thought – only we never had it and when we got Ellie back, Busta was in even more shit. Now he has to try and fit up someone else. Or give the money that he kept for himself back. He ain't gonna do that so we're still the number one targets. As far as Busta's boss is concerned we still have fifteen grand of his dough. And he wants it back.'

Nanny nodded again. 'So, tell me how Sally know all a dis? She work fe Busta?'

'No, but the other girl, Claire, is one of Busta's girls. Claire is Sally's best friend. She told her everything.'

'And weh dis gal, Claire?'

'I dunno. Sally told me that she thinks Busta has hurt her real bad. She kept telling me that Claire was dead.'

'Dead? Wha'? – murder we a deal wid too?'

'Well, she might be wrong, man. You know how people say someone's dead when what they really mean is that they are in trouble?'

'Might be . . .' He thought some more and then he smiled and slammed the table with his hands. 'Me have it! Yuh 'member de night we tek the money in?'

'Yeah?'

'When we approach the desk and de lickle Babylon ring de bigga Babylon upstairs?'

'Yeah,' I replied, wondering where Nanny was going with his story.

'When de one at de desk speak to the other one upstairs, him say, "Yes, one of them is IC3" – you remember, man?'

I thought hard, back to that night. My memory held all kinds of useless information in an easy access bank but more important stuff just faded away. I thought about what we had said to the copper on the desk that night and then it flooded back. Nanny was right. The unseen policeman had asked whether one of us was an IC3 male.

'IC3 is Babylon label fe de black man, nuh true?'

'Yeah, it is,' I agreed, recalling all those dodgy episodes of *The Bill*.

Nanny looked pleased with himself. 'Now, there was no other black man in de place so is how dat man upstairs can know that I man standing there? Unless him a . . .'

'Obeah man?'

'Yes, man!'

'So you're saying that the copper that interviewed us works for Busta's boss too?'

Nanny shrugged and then grinned. 'Mus' be, my yout'. Mus' be. I man don't see how him coulda known any other way. Dutty Babylon!'

'What was his name . . . ?' I asked, trying hard to remember.

Nanny just smiled. 'Me know him name,' he said. I marvelled at his feat of memory. I was shit at remembering

164

names. Maybe, I thought to myself, I should smoke as much weed as Nanny. Certainly didn't harm *his* brain that much. But then I realized I was being stupid – every spliff was probably killing like a million brain cells, man. Sack that.

'From when a Babylon have such a stupid name – I man can't forget it, y'know.'

'Nanny – what was his name?'

'*Rat*,' he said, smiling wide. 'Him name *Ratnett*.'

I smiled myself, amused by his name. How apt.

Suddenly Nanny jumped up shouting and cursing. '*Raas!* De bloodclaat food ruin nuh, man!' he said, picking up a dry, burnt and smoking pan.

twenty-eight:

wednesday,
5.30 p.m.

'And it was Busta crew dem who lock up Ellie?' We had moved to the living room and were sitting thinking things over. I had tried calling Della but my phone was out of credits and when I tried on my mum's land line, Della's phone was off anyway. I tried Jas's but his was on answer service so I assumed that they were together. I thought about calling Ellie and telling her to come round but the thought of frightening her didn't really appeal to me. She would find out soon enough anyway, along with the rest of the Crew. For now, I was better off letting Nanny in on everything that I knew. To tell the truth it was a weight off my shoulders and Nanny was the perfect person to share it all with. If anyone knew what to do it was Nanny – he was like our ghetto superstar.

In the background the telly was on, showing the latest instalment of *Neighbours*. Neither of us was watching it – there was a reggae CD playing and that took precedence over the TV. Dennis Brown was singing about it being 'too late' for him and his woman. The rhythm was underscored by a deep, heavy bass line. It was one of my mum's favourites.

'Nah, not his real crew, Sally said – just some man that he had working for him,' I replied, as I tapped my foot to the beat.

'And where is this man now?'

'Dunno. Sally said that Claire told her he was really creepy. Kept on making nasty comments about girls an' that.'

Nanny shook his head in disgust before changing the direction of the conversation. 'So Busta ah work fe Ratnett?'

'I'm not sure whether Ratnett is the actual boss but he's connected, I reckon.'

Nanny considered this for a moment and then spoke. 'And we only have one person word fe all a this?'

'Yeah, Sally.'

'So, even if we go to the police – dem nah believe we. Is one gal word against one of them own, man.'

'You reckon we should go to the police then?' I asked, wondering what other possible option was open to us. This was all getting too heavy.

'I man can find Busta – no problem, man. But if Ratnett involve in a dis then someone mus' inform de police.'

'Why?'

The thought of talking to the police made the hairs on my neck stand up. I knew that Nanny felt the same way too. That was why he had said '*someone*' should inform the coppers and not '*we*'.

'Because him have all de *power*, Billy. Him have de law 'pon him side.'

I thought about DI Elliot. Calling her was an option but why would Elliot believe us anyway? We were making serious allegations about one of her colleagues, without any real proof. *And* we had already lied to her once. Or at least not told her the whole truth. She was unlikely to investigate one of her own, regardless of her liberal copper speech. Her card was still in my pocket and I fished it out, handing it to Nan.

'This de woman police yuh a tell me about?'

'Yeah – the one that said she was on our side. Believe that,' I replied with a layer of sarcasm.

Neighbours had segued into the news and as we sat I looked at the screen, not really paying it too much attention. Then a headline for the local news caught my attention.

'Nanny! Turn down the CD, man.'

'Wha'?'

'Look – the telly! It's the community centre.'

On the screen an Asian reporter was talking in the foreground while, behind her, policemen searched the area to the side of the community centre – the car park where Will and I had argued with two of Busta's crew. The report switched to an interview and my stomach turned somersaults as I saw DI Elliot on the screen, her face downcast, a serious expression on it. I turned it up and listened, hoping that whatever had happened wasn't connected to us in any way. The thing was, I knew deep inside that it would be. It couldn't be just another coincidence because that would have been one too far.

'. . . *appealing for any information regarding this murder. The girl in question is too young to name but I can reveal that she was known locally as Claire. She may have been involved in prostitution and we believe she also had links to a local drug gang.'*

My stomach turned again and I ran out of the room into the kitchen, retching into the sink over and over. Nanny followed me and held my arms as I puked my guts out. When I stopped he guided me to the table and sat me down. I was shaking and shivering and my head was spinning.

'Jus' cool, Billy. Jus' cool,' said Nanny.

There was a knock on the back door and Della came hurrying in. When she saw how pale my face was she sat down opposite me and started to rub her hands together.

'You seen the telly then,' she said matter of factly.

I nodded and then cleared my throat. 'Yeah – it's her – it's Claire. The girl who was with . . .'

'Ellie? Yeah, I know. Me and Ellie have just seen the report on the news. Billy, we're in serious shit, man.'

'I know, Della.'

'We *gotta* call the police. You still got that card?'

'Yeah, it's in the living room. Can you get it for me? And where's Ellie?'

'Next door – she's well upset. I might get her to come round.'

'That's probably a good idea. And phone Jas and Will to warn them too.'

'Cool.'

'I'm gonna call DI Elliot.'

'Wait nuh, man!'

Della and me both turned to look at Nanny, wondering why he wanted us to wait. He was standing by the door with a serious look on his face. He came over and stood between the two of us. 'We need to give the Babylon somethin' to believe in nuh, man.'

Della shrugged her shoulders, and looked at me. 'Like what?' she asked.

I remembered that she didn't know what Nanny and I knew so I filled her in on Sally's revelations. As I spoke, Della sat and played with her hands. The longer my story went on, the more she fidgeted. It was a nervous reaction that I had seen in her before. She did it whenever she spoke about being a kid and what life with her parents had been like. She was scared. So was I.

Nanny stood, his chest wide and his chin up. 'Busta,' he said in a whisper. A whisper full of menace – not normal for Nanny. He was angry. I could tell.

'What you on about, Nanny?' I asked, confused by what he meant.

'I man will get de yout' to talk,' he replied, again in a whisper. 'We jus' need to find him firs'.'

'We?' Della and me spoke in unison.

'Yes, we, man. Call Jas and Will – mek we go find dat bwoi.'

'And then we'll call the police?' asked Della.

'Nah, man, just give we until midnight, princess. Tell the woman police to be here by then.'

'What if we don't find Busta?' I said. 'And even if we do – why is he gonna come along?'

Nanny smiled a sly smile. 'Yuh jus' leave dat to me, my yout',' he replied, his smile changing into serious intent.

I shivered slightly. Nanny was the calmest man I knew but I had never doubted his ability to be badder than the rest. I decided that I wouldn't swap places with Busta for a million pounds.

Not tonight.

twenty-nine:

wednesday, 6.30 p.m.

Nanny kept a list of important phone numbers written on the inner sleeve of a Gregory Isaac LP, *Night Nurse*. He had two copies of it, on vinyl rather than CD, and had pulled the one that he required from the racks of LPs in the cellar. My mum had converted the cellar – an area the same size as the ground floor and with a high ceiling – a few years earlier and it was like Nanny's den, the place where he kept his things. He had a sound system down there, part of a bigger set that he used to take around community centres across the country when I was younger. He had been part of a Rastafarian crew called Jah Steppers and his vinyl collection was massive.

Despite the number of records in the racks he knew exactly where everything was kept and it took him only moments to find the LP. He came back upstairs and started to ring round a few people, most of whom I didn't know. I waited until he had finished on the phone and then I spoke to Jas and Will. Will came straight round but Jas was at kick boxing and told us he would meet us later. I said that I'd text him with our whereabouts.

My mum got in around half-six. She had heard the report on the radio and was busy arguing with Nanny in the living room while the rest of us, minus Jas, waited in the kitchen. My mum was adamant that we had to call the police and risk the fact that they might not believe us. Her argument was that DI Elliot had already spoken to us about Claire, after Sally had been taken to hospital, and that she wasn't stupid. She would put two and two together soon enough, if she hadn't already.

Nanny had explained his reasoning to her, emphasizing the point that one copper wouldn't act on the word of a bunch of kids and a working girl. He told her that he could get Busta to talk, which was the best way to get the police to take us seriously. It wasn't like in the movies, he said. 'T'ings nah work so, baby,' he told her, as she went mad.

I was worried about them arguing but I was more concerned about Ellie. She looked scared and a couple of times I put my arm around her and tried to reassure her. She was worried that we'd get hurt going after Busta and wanted us to call the police straight away. Her parents hadn't yet heard the news about what had happened to the young girl, Claire, and she had decided not to tell them. Not until we had sorted out what we were going to do. All they had to do was turn on the TV and they'd find out soon enough, anyway.

For my part, I didn't have a clue what Nanny had planned but I knew that it involved some of his contacts, the people he had phoned. I had learned a few things about Nanny over the past week or so – some of them that maybe I wish I hadn't. I suppose we all have a history, hidden or not, but I wasn't about to hold Nanny's against him.

Will sat at the table, letting a cup of coffee go cold, fidgeting. I could tell that he was excited and apprehensive at the same time. I was too. The situation was reaching what my crime novel heroes would have called 'critical mass'. Breaking point. I was scared about going after Busta without telling the police but I was also ready to help Nanny. Busta had it coming and I was angry that it had been him who had been responsible for holding Ellie captive in that horrible old house. Over something that had nothing to do with us. Livid because we had spoken to him when we were looking for her and he'd just laughed. And that didn't even take Sally into account. Or Claire. Innocent working girls caught up in a stupid scam over money that had resulted in one of them ending up in hospital and the other one dead. I mean, how was the money worth someone's life? No amount of money equalled the life of a person. No amount. I got myself so worked up that I lit a fag.

'Them things are gonna kill you, Billy,' said Will.

'Sod it,' I replied, looking at Della, who shook her head in disgust at me.

'You ain't being big or clever,' she said, supporting Will. Normally it was Della and Will that were having a go at each other.

'And you'll end up smelling like an ashtray,' added Ellie.

'For f—'

I didn't finish my sentence, instead getting up and chucking the cigarette out of the kitchen door. The phone rang as I shut the door. I walked over to the wall where it hung and answered.

'Yeah, is Nanny there?' enquired the caller, a man whose voice could best be described as gravelly.

'He's in the other room. Who is it?' I wasn't in the mood to be polite.

'Ronnie. Tell him it's Ronnie Maddix.'

I let the phone hang and wondered how and why Nanny knew the caller. Ronnie Maddix was the biggest gangster in the city. The man that was behind everything, from doormen to cocaine. His was the kind of name that made people pay up their debts and leave town. He was a nutter. I went into the living room and told Nanny who it was. As soon as I mentioned the name he let out a groan, not because of who it was, but because I had told him in front of my mum. My mum's reaction confirmed it.

'RONNIE! What the hell are you doing calling that bastard?'

My mum rarely swore and when she did it was time to duck for cover. Nanny, to his credit or stupidity, chose to ignore her and said that he'd be back in a moment. As he left the room my mum turned on me.

'Are you *totally* stupid, Billy?'

'What?'

'Billy! Don't play me. Why the hell haven't you just called the police?'

I looked at her, seeing rage in her normally calm brown eyes, realizing that Nanny hadn't told her about the bent copper, Ratnett. 'There's something you don't know, Mum,' I said.

'And what is *that* exactly?' she said, all sarcastic and totally not like my mum.

But then again she *was* angry. I forgave her and then

told her everything that I had told Nanny. She listened wide-eyed and disbelieving until Nanny came back in and finished my story for me.

My mum considered things for a while after we had finished and then spoke in a quiet whisper. 'I'm assuming that Maddix is helping you find this Busta character?'

'Yes, man. Is what other reason me could have to call him?'

'The past is best left buried, Nan,' she said, leaving me wondering what she was talking about.

'The past is useful sometimes, Rita,' he replied.

She turned to look at me and then back to Nanny. 'You have until midnight – like you said. And you leave DI Elliot to me. Me and the girls. You aren't taking them out to play your testosterone-fuelled games.'

'Cool,' I said, hoping that Della would see it the same way and not smack me in the mouth.

'Listen, baby. I man nah go let the yout' dem get hurt. Is me yuh a deal wid.' Nanny was trying to reassure her.

'Yes, I know it's you. But it's a you that got left behind years ago and I don't want it back.'

I realized what they were on about. Nanny's old life. Nanny smiled a gentle, warm and caring smile and put his arms round my mum. He kissed her on the head and hugged her. 'I man just dust off an old coat, Rita. When me done me gonna put it back where it belong. *Jah know.*'

'Maybe *He* does,' conceded my mum. 'Just as long as you do too.'

I sent Jas a text around half-seven, telling him to meet us by the precinct near the community centre at nine. He'd

175

be safe there – there'd be loads of people around cos of Claire's murder; murder always brought out all the rubberneckers and gossips – Nanny called them the 'carry go bring comes'. He replied straight away – saying that he'd be there for half-nine, after kick boxing. My mum braved telling Della and Ellie that they were to wait with her. Ellie seemed quite relieved at the idea but Della complained and didn't stop until my mum spoke to her on her own. I don't know what she said to Della but my mum has a way with words, believe me. Nanny, Will and me left the house just gone eight, after another couple of calls from Ronnie Maddix.

Outside the night air was warm and the sounds of the ghetto rang in my ears as we walked into town, ready to meet with our city's answer to Public Enemy Number One. Nanny spoke little as we walked, his face fixed in a way that suggested he was determined to find Busta and make him talk. I looked at Will a few times and saw in his expression the same fear and excitement that I had. We were on a mission, man. A mission that I knew was going to be fun in a perverse way. Fun precisely because it would be so dangerous. My mum had been right about boys and testosterone.

thirty:

Wednesday, 8 p.m.

*D*ella was going mad until Billy's mum spoke to her and calmed her down. I don't know what she said to her but it worked. Now that Nanny and the lads had left the house Della kept going on about 'boys and testosterone' and how she wouldn't have slowed them down if they had taken her with them. 'I mean, ain't as if I can't handle myself, is it?'

I agreed with her – just to stop her from going off again. When Della threw a paddy, she really went for it. And that was the last thing I wanted. Billy's mum told me that we were going to have to tell my parents everything we knew. I didn't want to but she insisted, saying that it was wrong to keep them in the dark. The thing was – I didn't want to worry them. They had been through so much before when I'd been kidnapped, especially my mum. I didn't want to add to that. I mean, I'm a real sop when it comes to my family anyway. The smallest thing makes me cry. Once, Christopher fell over and cut his knee open and I cried for ages – not because I thought he would die or anything like that, but because I thought it would upset my mum. I know it's silly but then sometimes I am silly. How was I going to tell them that the girl who had been made to look after me when I was tied up had been murdered? A girl who was only about the same age as me.

They'd probably seen the telly by now anyway and that would make them worry to start with. What I had to tell them — well, that would just add to it.

In the end Billy's mum went round and got them, explaining everything, and then answering their questions about Sally, Claire and Busta. My mum reacted just as I had thought she would. She started to cry and that made me cry before my dad told us both not to worry. He asked Rita whether the police had been informed. Billy's mum said that she was going to call DI Elliot and outlined Nanny's plan to get Busta to talk. Then she told him about the policeman who was involved — Ratnett. That made my dad stop in his tracks. He sat and thought about things for a while before telling Rita that Nanny was right.

'I just hope he can get this Busta person to talk,' he told her.

'Don't worry, Brian — if anyone can get him to talk, it's Nanny,' she replied.

My dad looked at me and Della and then smiled. 'At least you two haven't gone with them,' he said.

Della was just about to start moaning again when I piped up, 'I know. Well, someone has to be here to do all the girlie things. Like make the tea.'

'And bake the buns?' added my dad, smiling.

'Ooh yes! Buns and cakes and pots of stew.' I was playing a game.

'Knock it off, Ellie,' said Della, trying to be serious but not managing to hold back a smile too.

'Oh, Della, don't be a grouchy old woman. Please?'

'Ellie . . .'

I pouted at her. 'I know — stop being silly. Is it any wonder you're always so angry?'

'I am not.'

'Yes you are.'

178

'No, I'm not!'

Billy's mum groaned. 'You two!'

Della and I exchanged glances and then burst out laughing. I know it wasn't the most normal thing to do in our situation – but there's that old saying, isn't there? You've got to make the best of a bad situation. My dad was always telling me that when life gave you lemons, the best thing to do was to make lemonade. That's what I was trying to do – make lemonade.

After a while I started wondering what Billy was doing and whether they had found Busta yet. It was half past nine when I looked at my phone to check the time and Billy's mum decided that she should call DI Elliot. She asked Della if she had seen the card with Elliot's number on it.

'It was just there,' replied Della, pointing at some random spot on the table where there was nothing at all.

'Oh, don't tell me Billy took it with him.'

'Knowing him,' said Della, 'he probably has.'

'Silly old man,' I added, grinning.

My dad told Rita not to worry and to call the station to get DI Elliot's number that way. They didn't have to bother. About ten minutes later the doorbell rang. Billy's mum went to answer it, then returned with DI Elliot right behind her.

'I thought I'd just drop round in the light of what's happened,' the policewoman was saying. She looked around, smiling when she saw me with my mum and dad and then turning back to Billy's mum. 'There's a few things I need to ask you. About the girl who your son found beaten up. And about some other things, too.'

Billy's mum looked at me and then Della. 'I think you had better sit down,' she told DI Elliot. 'You're not going to like this . . .' And she began to tell DI Elliot exactly what Nanny and Billy had told her . . .

thirty-one:

wednesday, 9 p.m.

Ronnie Maddix was waiting for us outside a bar in the city centre. It was one of the twenty or so bars and clubs where his door firm ran the bouncers and he was easy to spot. He was scary to look at. Six feet four inches of muscles and no neck at all. He was a monster. I had always thought of Will as big, but if there had been a gold medal for size given out that night, it would have gone to Ronnie. Nanny told me and Will to hang back so that he could speak to Ronnie alone. No way were we going to complain when we saw the size of Nanny's friend.

Will whistled. 'Bwoi, he is one big mofo, man.'

'You can say that again, Will,' I replied. 'He makes you look like a baby, my dread.'

'Hey – he ain't *that* big, you know.'

I looked at Will incredulously. 'Get lost, man! He's twice the size of you!'

Will mumbled under his breath but didn't bother to challenge my assertion. He couldn't.

As Nanny reached him, Ronnie gave him a bear hug, smothering Nanny so that all that remained in sight were his dreads. He let go, looked Nanny up and down, then hugged him again. Eventually they walked away from the door and the prying ears of the other doormen and spoke quietly together.

Will turned to me, puzzled. 'What's up there then?' he asked.

'How d'you mean, man?'

'Nanny and Maddix? I didn't know Nanny knew them kinda people.'

I didn't know what to tell Will. I had no idea that Ronnie Maddix and Nanny were mates either and, let's face it, Nanny was my dad to all intents and purposes. 'I dunno how they know each other,' I replied eventually. 'Ask him, man.'

'Who – Nanny or Maddix?' asked Will.

'The one that scares you the least,' I said, smiling.

'Very funny, you wanker.'

We waited for another five minutes or so, not exchanging another word. Nanny took something from Ronnie and put it in his pocket – a piece of paper or something similar – and came back over to us.

Ronnie watched him and then followed. He looked from me to Will and grinned before speaking in his distinct tone. 'Awright, lads? How's tricks then?'

'All right,' I said, looking at Nanny. Will just shrugged and nodded his head.

Ronnie let out a gruff laugh. 'It's cool, lads – I ain't gonna hurt yer. Your man there,' he started, nodding in Nanny's direction, 'is an old friend of mine. Brother, you could say.'

'Yeah, man,' laughed Nanny. 'We get we stripes together nuh, man.'

'At Her Majesty's Pleasure – numbers 54 an' 46' added Ronnie, talking about some old ska tune Nanny had. 54–46 was a prison number. He gave me a funny look and then turned to Nanny. 'This Rita's kid?' he asked, nodding at me this time.

Nanny looked at me, as if to ask permission. I shrugged. 'Yeah, man, him call Billy.'

'Billy,' repeated Ronnie. He looked away for a split second and then put his huge arm round my shoulder. 'I know yer old man, son. Lynden. Works with me.'

I looked at him and edged away. I hadn't seen my old man in years and he hadn't bothered to come see me. The fact that he worked with Ronnie Maddix washed right over me. 'Lucky you,' I said, hoping that he wouldn't take offence.

I had nothing to worry about. He just laughed out loud and hugged me to him. 'Just like yer mam, in't yer? Lots of bottle.'

I waited until he let me go before I could take my next breath.

'Him cool, Ronnie,' said Nanny. 'How dat bwoi, Lynden?'

'Same old Lynden, man. I'll give him your regards,' replied Ronnie, looking at me and raising his eyebrow.

Despite what I said, the thought of saying at least a hello to my old man was exciting, although it was tempered by a feeling of guilt that I had because of Nanny. I didn't want to hurt his feelings. Nanny read my mind.

'Yuh tell dat bwoi him pickney say hello. Tell him come check fe him soon.'

'I'll make sure of it,' smiled Ronnie.

'Right, we gone,' declared Nanny.

Ronnie put his massive, gold-ringed hand on Nanny's shoulder. 'Remember, dread, anything you need. If you need me to come with yer ...'

'Nah, it cool, Ronnie. If I need yuh I man will call.'

'You sure? I mean, it's no bother. Might be a laugh.'

At that Will looked at me and frowned. The man really was a nutter.

'Nuh worry yuhself, Ronnie. Jus' tek care, y'hear? Respec', bredda.'

'Yeah, respec' and all that. Although I can never understand that Jamaican you speak, mate. You never talked that way at school.'

Nanny laughed along with his friend and then we set off for the community centre. Back to the ghetto.

On the way I sent Jas a text, confirming that we were on our way to the centre. He didn't reply but then I hadn't expected him to. We walked back over the ring road, via the bridge and into the heart of the two huge estates that made up one half of the ghetto. On every corner there were gangs of kids and older crews hanging around or dealing in five-pound bags of weed. Some of the kids smoked cigarettes and spliffs and one or two had cans of super strong lager in their hands. If we hadn't been on a mission, I'm sure Nanny would have lectured them about the perils of alcohol and that – but we had somewhere to go, someone to see. Further along, a lad who couldn't have been more than twelve tried to sell Will a mobile phone. Will gave him a look that sent the lad running back to the badly lit stairwell where his mates stood watching. Even in the dim light I could make out an older lad, urging his charges to go out and earn him a living. People like that were all over our area – like predators, ready to bite at the first opportunity.

We reached the community centre just after quarter to ten but Jas hadn't arrived. The side of the centre, by the car park, had been blocked off with police tape. The fluorescent yellow strips stood out under the streetlights and around them stood more gangs of kids, looking at the spot where another local had become an overnight star. Most of them had probably seen Claire around the streets – some probably knew her. One or two might even know what had happened to her and who had done it. But not a single one would have spoken to the police, other than to cuss them and call them names. That was the state of things. Nanny used to call it the 'writing on the wall'. It was an indication of the times in which we had to live. Sad but true.

I snapped back to the matter in hand and rang Jas, only to be told that I had run out of credits on my phone. Will got his out, but he had no credit either. The only option was a phone box, although finding one that worked was a mission in itself. Nanny fiddled for something in his jacket and pulled out a mobile.

I looked at him, astonished. 'Where'd you get that?' I asked, pointing at the phone.

'Me just have it, man. Lying around.'

'But you're always banging on about how mobiles rot your brain and that!'

'Is fe emergency use only, man.'

I grinned. 'But surely it's a fruit of Babylon?' I said, winding him up.

'Rest yuhself, Billy. Babylon nah have no fruit.'

Will started laughing. 'Never mind about Babylon, Nanny. If that was my phone, I'd hide it too! It's a brick, man!'

It was true. Nanny's phone was twice the size of mine and looked like the sort of thing you got when you first signed up for one. Wack. Nanny frowned. 'At least me have credit 'pon mine,' he said.

'I'd rather hunt for a working phone box,' I said, still grinning.

'Jus' call Jas nuh, man! We don't have time to mess about.'

Nanny was right, of course. I dialled Jas's number and waited. The connection took ages and when it did hook up with Jas's phone, the answer service came on. 'He must be on his way,' I said. 'It's on answer.'

'Then we better wait fe him,' replied Nanny, sitting down on the steps of the community centre and taking his phone back from me.

Nanny dialled up someone that he called Tek Life, speaking for a brief few moments. As he put his brick back in his pocket a young Asian lad on a mountain bike rode up to us. He looked at me and Will and then at Nanny. 'Which one of you guys is Billy?' he asked, his face all serious.

I moved towards him. 'I am,' I said. 'What do you want?'

'I don't want nuttin' from you, guy.' Pure attitude. Attitude that disappeared when Will grabbed him by the collar. 'Hey! Hey! Leave me alone, man!' squealed the kid, trying to get loose.

'What do you want?' I asked again, getting a bad feeling in my stomach.

'Man jus' tol' me to give you dis letter, you know.' He handed over an envelope.

I tore it open and pulled out a sheet of A4 paper. I read it and then grabbed the kid by the throat. 'WHO GAVE YOU THIS?'

The kid tried to talk but couldn't until I let him go. I handed the letter to Will and then grabbed the kid again, this time by his jacket, slapping his baseball cap off his head. 'Tell me, you little—'

'Weren't me, man! Some white guy gave it me. Told me to wait for you lot. It's nuttin' to do with me, man. He just give me a fiver to deliver it – I swear that's the truth!'

'What white man?' I shouted, as Nanny read the letter too.

'Dunno! Just some man, innit.'

I let the kid go and looked at Will and Nanny. The letter told us that someone had Jas and said that I would be next – unless I came up with the money. My mind was going haywire. Who had Jas and what had happened to him? This was serious. First Ellie and now Jas. The Crew was in deep, man. I shivered as I remembered Claire. They had already killed her. What would stop them from doing the same to Jas. Just the thought nearly made me puke.

Nanny kept his cool and asked the Asian kid which way the man had gone and whether he'd seen Jas. The kid, who was shaking by now, said that the man who gave him the letter had just driven off in a black car. He hadn't seen anyone else. Nanny told the kid to get lost and turned to face me and Will, both of us fuming.

'Tek Life will be here in a minute. We best find Busta quick time.'

186

'I'm gonna break his neck when we do,' said Will. He meant it too.

'I'd better let Mum know,' I said, but Nanny told me to leave it for a while.

'Mek we get dat bwoi first,' he said, meaning Busta.

We stood in silence, waiting for Nanny's friend. Will was pacing, one way and then another, finally walking over to the door of the community centre and unleashing a punch so powerful that it cracked the wood. At the same time he let out a grunt, then calmly walked back over to us. He stared at me and Nanny, a look of madness and rage glinting in his eyes. 'That's it,' he said in a whisper. 'Somebody's got to pay.'

thirty-two:

wednesday, 10 p.m.

Tek Life showed up in a BMW with blacked-out windows. The electric whirr of his window gave way to clouds of smoke from his spliff as he grinned a gold-toothed smile at us. A deep, rolling bass line provided him with a mobile soundtrack. 'Irie, Nanny – what up, man?'

'Bad t'ings a gwan, y'know. Busta and him boss have one of we yout' dem.'

Tek Life looked at me and Will. 'Well, you best get in, my yout's.'

The drive to Busta's yard took about ten minutes. His actual house wasn't in the ghetto but on a predominantly white estate on the other side of the ring road. Tek Life's car was like a death trap for asthmatics, the thick, acrid smoke of his spliff making my eyes water. But I didn't mind too much. I didn't care in fact. My mind was racing with possibilities and probabilities about who had Jas and what they would do to him. I was gutted. First Ellie and now Jas – by the *same* people – the people who had beaten Sally and killed Claire. I wasn't too comfortable about not telling Jas's mum either. We *had* to. What if something happened to him? She wouldn't ever forgive us if Jas got badly hurt and she found out that we had held back. I wanted to talk to Nanny, but he was busy telling Will why his friend had the nickname that he had.

'See, my man here – his real name Patrick but in the dance we call him Tek Life.'

'Why? What does Tek Life mean anyway?'

'Exactly what it say nuh, man. Him take life.'

Will suddenly looked all scared. 'What, he's a murderer?'

Tek Life let out a low, rumbling laugh that sounded like an earthquake.

'No, man.' Nanny grinned. 'See, Patrick was lazy back in those days. He used to jus' sit 'pon the stage and never dance until his favourite tune play. And then – man, yuh could never stop him. Him jump up and throw out him legs and him arms like a ninja.'

'Oh, right.' Will still looked none the wiser.

'And the selector – what de yout' man call the DJ nowadays – him know exactly which tune Patrick did love. So every time he play dem tune, him shout out, "Patrick? TEK LIFE!"'

'And the name stuck,' grinned Patrick. 'Like superglue.'

I let them talk, understanding that for both Will and Nanny talking about something, anything, stopped them from doing what I was doing – running things over and over in my head. Driving myself spare. Who was to say which method was the right one in dealing with what had happened to Jas? Certainly not me.

We drove back through the ghetto, past dealers on street corners and takeaways and working girls. Every so often a police car would float past us and the occupants would scrutinize Patrick's car, wondering who was driving it and to what end. There were kerb-crawlers slowing our progress through the streets and stupid kids riding out in front of the car on mountain bikes sprayed in garish yellows and greens. Outside a small mosque, a group of Muslim men were talking, while across the road from them an Asian youth stood with a mobile in each hand, taking orders and making deals. We crossed the front-line area and as the car passed a couple of the alleyways that ran from it, crack dealers emerged from the shadows, removing their merchandise from its hiding place in their mouths, thinking that we were looking for a rock or two.

I had seen a play on the telly once – a version of Dante's *Inferno* – and I wondered what the writer would have made of my area after dark, when all the creeps came out to play. My mood was hardly alleviated by the music playing on Patrick's car stereo either. Dread reggae music warning vampires and evil-doers to beware of an impending Armageddon, all underscored by powerful, hypnotic bass notes and crashing cymbals. The smoke from Patrick's spliff was putting me in a daze, making my mind wander from pillar to post without finding a single coherent thought.

I could hear Nanny and Patrick talking but I wasn't actually listening to them. I was wondering how Busta would react when we got to his place – assuming that he was at home, that is. I wished we were already there instead of on the way because the tension inside my body was building and my stomach was churning again. I hadn't eaten anything since I had found out about Claire so there was nothing to throw up, but the feeling of nausea was far more unsettling than the actual act of puking, which was at least a release. Yet when Nanny broke my thoughts by telling me that we had reached the street where Busta lived, I suddenly remembered something that my teachers at school always said to me, whenever I told them that I hated the place and didn't want to be there. They told me to be careful what I wished for. If I had thought that my tense feeling would disappear when we got to Busta's, I was wrong. It got worse.

Busta lived in a low-rise council block. Patrick told us that one of his girlfriends lived in the same block so he knew it well and could get us in, even though it had a key-card entry system for added security. 'My gal give me a spare card so I can check for her any time,' he said with another toothy grin.

We got out of his car and waited whilst he went to the boot to get something. He returned with a sledgehammer about a metre long and encrusted with dried concrete. I just looked at him.

'Don't you think we'll be a touch conspicuous if you're carrying that?' Will pointed at the sledgehammer.

Patrick just grinned on. 'Nuh worry yuhself. I ain't never had no bother before.'

Before? I didn't even want to guess at what Tek Life did for a living. Man, how did Nanny know all these dodgy blokes?

We made our way to a door beyond which was a dimly lit stairwell and Patrick ran a plastic card about the size of a credit card through a machine on the wall. The red light on the machine changed to green and the sound of bolts unlocking echoed in the stairwell. He pushed the reinforced glass door open and ushered us inside. Taking the lead, he ran up the steps two at a time as we made for the top floor.

'Ronnie tol' me that him live in twenty-t'ree,' explained Nanny as we hit the top floor and walked down a dimly lit corridor. 'Seventeen, nineteen, twenty-one. Ah! We have it nuh, man.'

Flat twenty-three had a dirty, yellowing door. From within the thumping bass of a garage tune could be felt. Nanny put his finger to his lips, asking us to keep quiet, something that I found very strange considering that Busta had his music on so loud. That, and of course the fact that we were about to break his door down with a sledgehammer. Better not sneeze, I thought to myself. We might alert him to our presence.

Nanny put his ear to the door and then gestured for Patrick to swing his hammer. The door broke open with one swing and a thunderous crack. Nanny went flying through, followed by Patrick and then Will. I looked up and down the corridor, checking to see if anyone would come out to see what the noise was. No one did, which in itself said something about the area we were in.

Inside Nanny ran through a living room and headed for a door to the left of it, a door that had just slammed shut. He shoulder barged it open as the rest of us followed. I was the last one into Busta's bedroom and in the time it took me to get through the door, Nanny and Patrick had already got Busta in a hold and had him pushed against his own bed. Busta was wearing a leather outfit, trousers and shirt, with gold dripping from his neck – ghetto not-so-fabulous. His face, light brown and freckled, was screwed up – looking for an explanation. Some UK garage stars were singing about how no one knew about their crew and I thought about how Busta didn't know about ours – he was in shock, man, struggling underneath Nanny. He was going nowhere.

I looked around the room. In one corner, next to the bed, was a table. On it was a plastic money bag full of white powder. Patrick left Busta to Nanny and went over to the table, picking up the bag. He sniffed the contents, then dipped in his finger, tasting it. Grinning again, he turned to Busta, who was still wriggling. 'You are temporarily out of business,' he told him, pocketing the bag.

Underneath the table I spotted another bag, a bigger one – a black nylon holdall, just like the one that Will and Jas had found. I went over and grabbed it. Inside was a large amount of money. The second bag. I turned to the others. 'It's the rest of the money,' I told them.

Nanny let Busta sit up but kept his head in an armlock.

'Bwoi, yuh not very clever,' said Patrick, pointing at the bag. 'Yuh could'a try to hide de money at least. Is what kinda criminal yuh call yuhself?'

'Look like yuh have a lickle explainin' to do, man. Where we friend at?' added Nanny.

Busta struggled a bit more, stopping when he realized it was useless. Nanny had him strong. He swore.

'Hush yuh mout', bwoi!' shouted Nanny, in a tone that I had never heard him use. Man, it scared *me*. Lord only knows what it did to the state of Busta's boxer shorts.

Patrick leaned into Busta's face and then pulled some gold from his neck in a sudden movement. He looked at the chains and smiled. 'Busta, I think it's time you told us what a gwan, yes? An' quickly. Where de kid at?'

Busta swore again. Patrick slapped him. Busta spat blood.

Nanny looked at me. 'Call Rita,' he told me, handing me his brick again. I didn't need telling twice. 'Tell her about Jas – and tell her to call de Babylon. We bringin' dem a nonce, man.'

At the mention of the police, Busta started to struggle again, kicking out his legs like a dying fly. From nowhere Will flew in with a punch that took out two of Busta's teeth. 'You best hope my man is OK,' he told a distraught Busta. 'Or there's only you and me gonna square it. And I ain't in the mood to play no more,' he finished, just as my mum answered the phone.

thirty-three:

wednesday, 11 p.m.

'Where is he? Where?' Jas's mum was waiting for us by the time we got back to the house. She opened the door to us in tears, grabbing hold of Nanny.

'Where is he, Nanny?'

Nanny looked at his feet. 'Me nuh know. He was gonna meet us by the centre but him never show up.'

'Oh God!' She turned to me and Will.

'I'm sorry,' I told her. 'We thought he was coming to meet us after kick boxing but . . . we just got *this* . . .' I handed her the note and she burst into fresh tears.

My mum was standing behind Jas's mum. She looked really angry, making me wish I had just called the police straight after the Asian kid had told us his news. Patrick had stayed in his car, keeping an eye on Busta, who he had tied up with some electrical wire, and staying out of DI Elliot's way.

The kitchen felt like a railway station waiting room with so many faces sitting around the table, waiting for something that wasn't about to arrive. Ellie and her parents were there, along with Della and Sue. There was

195

a policeman in uniform and next to him Lucy Elliot, wearing the sort of look that suggested we were in a lot of trouble. She gestured for the uniform to go outside.

'Where is this Busta?'

'He's in the car,' I told her, looking at Nanny.

'And he's talking, is he?'

Nanny nodded. 'Yeah, yuh could say that.'

'Meaning what exactly?' Elliot eyed Nanny and then me with the kind of suspicious look that only a copper can give you.

'Him tell we everything. 'Bout kidnap and drugs and ting.' Nanny shrugged as he finished speaking as if to say, 'It's up to you what you do now.'

Elliot turned to the uniform. 'Right, get PC Raines from the car and take the suspect down to Central.'

'Yes, ma'am,' replied the young copper, with genuine fear in his face. He looked scared of Elliot.

It was only when she looked at me that I realized why. Her eyes were blazing. Not looking at the PC, she told him what to charge Busta with. 'Kidnap, attempted murder and murder,' she said, as though each thing meant nothing to her.

'Yuh want I fe get de bwoi from de car, miss?' asked Nanny, actually being polite.

'Yes,' replied Elliot. 'And then I'd like to see all three of you and your friend with the car in your living room, if you don't mind.'

The last part was directed at my mum, who nodded. 'Be my guest, Lucy,' she said. Lucy? So my mum was getting friendly with the Babylon now? Talk about loyalty. The look on my face was a big mistake. My mum spat out her words. 'And you, Billy, can keep your views to yourself. I can't believe you didn't phone the police straight away.'

'But Mum – I was going to—'

'Just get in that living room and be grateful that you haven't been arrested. Yet,' she said, turning away.

'Arrested for what?' asked Will, looking directly at Elliot.

She didn't even blink. 'How about obstructing a police investigation for starters?' she said.

'Get stuffed, man! Without us, you wouldn't have nothing. Man, we just went and *got* you the effin' suspect, you dutty . . .'

'William! *Shut up!*' My mum's voice cut through the room and shut Will up.

'Without you and your pretend detective friends we wouldn't have a missing young man either,' added Elliot.

I looked at my mum, then at Jas's and over to Ellie and Della, who were surprisingly quiet, especially Della. No support from anywhere. I turned to Elliot. 'Listen, Babylon – we didn't kidnap no one and we didn't kill no one and we sure as hell ain't to blame for this mess, all right?'

'I'm sorry,' replied Elliot sincerely. 'I just need to know exactly what has been going on. This *is* a murder enquiry – not to mention another abduction.'

'Well, perhaps you had better speak to one of your colleagues.'

'If you are talking about DI Ratnett, I *know*. Your mother told me.'

I looked at her in surprise.

'Ratnett has been under investigation for six months. We know about him,' she continued.

'What? And you just let him carry on?' asked Will. 'Instead of using him to catch his boss?'

Elliot sighed and her face softened. 'We think Ratnett *is* the boss,' she said.

Everyone in the room suddenly sat up and listened.

'*He's* the man your friend Busta works for. He's behind it all.'

Nanny walked back into the kitchen as Elliot spoke. He looked at her. 'My associate haffe leave to go a work,' he told her, talking about Tek Life. 'But I have de money here.' He handed the nylon bag over to Elliot.

She raised an eyebrow and then shrugged.

'It's Ratnett – the policeman,' said Ellie's dad, in Nanny's direction. 'That's who's behind all of this. Was it him who kidnapped Ellie too?'

Nanny shook his head. 'No, Brian – Sally told Billy it was Busta organize the kidnap – some man him know.'

'And where is this *man* now?' asked Elliot.

'Him gone. Busta coulda tell yuh where him deh.'

Nanny's reply confused Elliot – which he saw and then corrected.

'Busta–can–tell–yuh–where–the–man–is,' he reiterated s-l-o-w-l-y.

Jas's mum started to cry again, hugging my mum, as Elliot brushed her hands down the skirt she was wearing. She took out her mobile and rang someone. Her boss. She spoke for a few moments, telling whoever was on the other end of the line about Jas and Busta and everything else we had told her.

'I've sent the suspect in for questioning,' she said. The voice on the other end was male and loud. 'Yes, sir, I've arranged for that. Only yourself and the Chief are allowed near him.' There was more of the loud male voice. 'Yes, sir. I'll call back in twenty minutes. With all due respect, sir, I think I can handle things my end.'

She flipped her phone shut just as her boss began to reply and turned to face me and Will. Putting the phone in her bag she mouthed the word 'wanker' to us, meaning her boss, smiled and then asked us to follow her into the living room. Nanny came with us. Behind me my mum was still comforting Jas's mum and Ellie had started sobbing. I couldn't believe what was going on – it was surreal, like one of those dreams where everyone you know is part of the action but the actual situation makes no sense. My mum's house was like the drop-in centre *and* police interview room. The coppers were the criminals and me, Will and Nanny were the detectives. And to top it all, Della hadn't gone mad and Ellie wasn't talking about random stuff. It had to be a dream.

Between myself, Nanny and Will, we managed to tell DI Elliot everything that had happened. We told her about the money, the first kidnap, the assault on Jas, the warnings, everything. We told her about how Claire had used Sally as a go-between to tell us where Ellie was being held and how there had been a second bag of money which we had found at Busta's – the bag Nanny had brought in. I explained my visit to Sally and how she had told me all about Busta and his scam. Elliot was upset at that because she had tried to get Sally to talk and hadn't managed it.

'She doesn't trust the police,' I said.

'Can't really blame her, can you?' added Della with a large dollop of sarcasm.

Elliot just shrugged. 'Like I said before, Billy. There's good and bad police.' It was a bad move on her part.

'All I ever seen is bad,' replied Della. She stood up and went over to the window. 'See, DI Elliot, you don't get it round here. *No one* likes the police because they've learned the hard way that Babylon can't be trusted. So when things get messed up, we turn to each other. I would rather let Nanny help me out than you because he knows what he's doing . . .'

'But—' began Elliot.

'Nah, man, let me finish. If you lose something round here, or you wanna find someone, it's better to ask the kids on the mountain bikes and the dealers and those poor cows that work over by the church and that. We don't need no community police round this way 'cos we police ourselves, up to a point. *Yeah* – the dealers and the pimps just go about their business – but so what?'

'What about authority?'

'Authority? I look up to my mum and Billy's mum and the rest of the Crew. I look up to Nanny and his mates, and the women who have worked them streets for years just to send their kids to school with full bellies. I don't look up to you and your institutions, man. For *what*?'

'I know it's hard,' said Elliot, looking almost sad. Man, she was definitely strange for a copper. She was sympathetic.

'Nah, you don't know. To most of you coppers this is a no-go zone. Most of 'em don't give a shit. They patrol because they have to.'

'Yeah, man,' agreed Nanny. 'If all a dis dealin' and slavery of woman a gwan in your middle-class area then it would get close down dead. But from when it contain in de ghetto . . .'

'. . . then your institutions and your police don't give a monkey's,' finished Della, wiping a tear away.

Elliot knew that she wasn't about to change anyone's mind and to her credit she stopped trying. See, in the ghetto, Elliot – if she was as sincere as she seemed – was an anomaly, an aberration. She wasn't par for the course and that was the real problem. Della and me and the rest of the Crew – even Ellie, who hadn't always lived here – could see what was going on. We saw the good and we saw the bad and we weren't stupid. Only coppers and teachers and social workers who told us things were getting better – only they were stupid. Because they were telling lies to people who already lived the truth.

The interview had drifted into a debate almost – until Mr Sykes pulled us all back into focus. 'Are we gonna sit round and talk bloody sociology or are we gonna *do* something to find Jas? Poor lad could be dead.'

'Let me call my boss back,' replied DI Elliot, looking a little embarrassed. 'See where we've got to.'

'Nothing like gettin' yer priorities right,' added Ellie's dad, with sarcasm and just a touch of anger.

thirty-four:

wednesday, midnight

DI Elliot spent about twenty minutes on the phone to her boss and by that time it was getting close to midnight. As soon as she got off the phone she went into the kitchen and spoke to Jas's mum. I stood with her as she spoke. Apparently Busta had offered to give evidence against Ratnett without even being asked. The police had threatened him with a child kidnap, murder and abuse charge and that had scared him silly. I knew why too. Busta would gladly have done time for a normal crime – getting sent down was a rite of passage in the ghetto, a way to get respect. But doing time on a *child abduction* charge? On the nonce wing? Forget it. Busta would be finished.

They still had no clue where Jas was – only that Ratnett was involved. And Busta was prepared to help, in return of course for some lesser charges against him. Their plan was to get Busta to call Ratnett and tell him that we had given him the second bag. Busta would then arrange a meeting with Ratnett to hand over the money and hopefully find out where Jas was being held. The whole thing would be taped so it could be played back to Ratnett when he was arrested. A classic sting operation, as my crime novel heroes would have put it.

Jas's mum sat and thought about it, telling Elliot that she didn't care what they did as long as Jas was safe. She told her that all she wanted was for her son to come back in one piece and not end up like Claire. Elliot reassured her that the operation was a top priority and would happen almost immediately. As soon as Busta had been wired up and briefed.

'We won't allow it to drag into tomorrow,' said Elliot. 'It's too much of a risk.'

Jas's mum shuddered at the word 'risk'.

Elliot then turned to me. 'Well, that's all I'll be needing from you,' she said quietly.

'What?'

'Obviously I'll need you to fill out proper statements and possibly testify – once we arrest Ratnett and put him on trial. But as far as playing the detective . . . leave that to me.'

'But Jas is part of *our* crew,' I protested.

'Yes, I know,' she replied patiently. 'And the best thing you can do for him is to stay at home and let us find him. We *will* find him.'

'Like you found Ellie, you mean?'

Lucy Elliot gave me a look that said, Don't push it. I didn't.

My mum stepped in and agreed with her. 'You've done enough, Billy,' she said. 'Busta is in custody and Ratnett is about to be arrested too.'

'But Jas—'

'Jas will be fine,' she said, smiling. 'DI Elliot will make sure of that, won't you?' She looked at Elliot.

'Yes. I will *personally* make sure of it.'

'Yeah, right,' I said, resigned to the fact that our little adventure was over.

'Look, Billy – thanks for your help. I just can't allow myself to put any of you in danger. This is serious. As far as we know, Ratnett is desperate – he's already implicated in the murder of one person. I can't risk anyone else. It's against my ethical and professional judgement.'

'You mean it's more than your job's worth?'

'Yes, it is. I didn't slog my way to where I am just to throw it away,' said Elliot. She meant it too.

Zeus, who had disappeared upstairs earlier because of the number of people in the house, reappeared with a sheepish look on his face and stood by the door, whining.

'He needs to go outside,' said Ellie.

'Has anyone walked him?' I asked, looking around.

'Yes, Billy,' replied my mum. 'In between finding out about a murder, losing Jas and having half of the street in the kitchen, someone managed to take him out.' Sarcasm of the highest order.

'Billy, Billy – dissed by your own mother!' said Will, which made everyone grin. Even my mum.

She looked at me with a smile. '*Well?* It was a stupid thing to ask,' she said.

'Thanks, Mum,' I replied, mildly annoyed.

'I'll take him,' offered Della suddenly.

'Della, it's after midnight,' said Sue.

'Well just let him out into the yard,' added my mum.

Will stood up and yawned. He looked at Della and then Ellie. Turning to my mum, he told her that he'd go out there with the girls. He grabbed Zeus's lead from a hook above his basket and opened the back door. Zeus didn't need a second invitation, bounding out into the yard. Not bad for a dog you normally had to drag out of his basket.

Della looked at me. 'You coming?'

'Nah,' I replied, yawning.

'OK,' replied Della with a sad look in her eyes.

'Dell, take your phone with you. Just in case,' I said.

'Just in case what? You think with half the police force having visited your house tonight that anyone is stupid enough to try anything? In the back yard?'

'No, but just to be sure.'

Della's eyes frosted over. 'Let them come, Billy. Mood I'm in – a bwoi's gonna get a kickin' anyways.'

Looking at her face, I could well believe it. But she picked up her phone anyway, her beautiful feline features set in a serious way.

thirty-five:

thursday, 00.45 a.m.

The phone rang just after quarter to one in the morning. I was in the kitchen with my mum, Nanny and Sue.

'Yeah, can I speak to Nanny?' The caller was Ronnie Maddix – no one else had that voice.

'Hang on a minute, Ronnie,' I replied, 'I'll just get him.'

The conversation lasted about ten minutes, with Nanny listening mostly. I sat down next to my mum and waited for him to finish.

My mum looked at Sue. 'I wonder what he wants now,' she said.

Sue shrugged. 'Ronnie Maddix,' she said quietly. 'Now there's a blast from the proverbial.'

I wondered whether I should mention what Ronnie had told me about my biological father but decided that it would be the last thing my mum would want to hear right now. Anyway, he was history, so why bring him up? My mum told Sue about his earlier call and Sue's eyes grew wider.

'Is he still in the same game?' she asked my mum, who nodded.

'People like him never change.'

'I don't get it,' said Sue. 'What does he have to do with all of this?'

'He told us where to find Busta,' I replied.

'Ah – the ghetto grapevine,' smiled Sue.

'Do you *all* know him then?' I asked.

My mum and Sue looked at each other. 'We did, once. Long time ago, kid.'

Sue agreed with my mum. 'People like him are best left in the past,' she said.

'Well, he did us a favour,' I replied. Bad move.

'Ronnie doesn't do anyone a favour unless there's something in it for him,' snapped my mum.

'Your mum's right, Billy. He's not the kind of man you want to owe anything to. Monetary or otherwise.'

I thought about what they were saying and then shrugged it off. I didn't care what Maddix did – all I knew was he had helped us out and that was fine by me. I didn't owe him anything, anyway. He didn't have to help.

Nanny put the phone down and came back to the table. My mum eyed him suspiciously. 'Is it payback time already?' she asked.

'Nah, baby – nuttin' like that.' He sat down and scratched his bearded chin.

'So – what did he want?' asked my mum sternly.

'Him find one of Busta bwoi dem. The bwoi tell him where Ratnett deh.'

'*What?*' My mum looked at Nanny in disbelief.

'Ronnie just told me where Ratnett holdin' Jas. Him a watch de place – seh him have a plan. I man ago meet him.'

'Ronnie knows where Jas is?' I added. 'And we can go get him?' Nanny nodded. I realized that something wasn't quite right with what Nanny was telling us. 'How did Ronnie know about Jas?' I asked.

We hadn't even known about Jas's abduction when we'd met Maddix and we certainly hadn't told him that Ratnett was Busta's boss. After all, we'd only found *that* out when we had come back to the house. *After* speaking to Maddix. A long while after.

Nanny looked a little sheepish. 'Listen, Ronnie a run t'ings. Him know about the dodgy policeman already.'

'So why didn't he tell you?' asked my mum, getting angry.

'Because I tol' him we want Busta. I never even mention de police.'

'But he *must* have known that Busta and Ratnett were connected. He *had* to, man. Like you just said – Ronnie knows everything.'

Nanny looked at me and nodded.

My mum sighed. 'I give up,' she said. 'This is getting too stupid for words. Call the police, Nanny. This is a child's *life* we're talking about.'

'OK, mek yuh call the Babylon an' tell them,' he said to my mum. 'But me nuh ina dat, man.'

'You're scared of what Ronnie might think?' she asked, sighing again.

Nanny shook his head. 'Listen, from when man t'ink I man a grass – me can't stay round here.'

Nanny had a point. Right or wrong, where we lived, being labelled an informer was the worst thing that could happen. Especially to someone like Nanny. It could make life dangerous for him. It was all right helping the police to get Busta – he had kidnapped one child and helped kill another. The whole thing about informing didn't apply to nonces – they got what was coming to them. Busta was *lucky* that the police had him. In our neighbourhood anyone that messed with a kid got wasted, man. It was simple, black and white, ghetto logic.

But telling them what *Maddix* had planned – that was different. Ronnie was *the* man, not to mention a friend of Nanny's. He couldn't grass him up. No way. Where would that leave Nanny? The next time a crack dealer got busted or the police closed down some pimp's operation, the finger would point at Nanny automatically. That was the way things worked. And my mum knew it. Nanny was in an impossible situation. Rock and a hard place style. It was the life we lived in.

'DI Elliot told us that Busta was going to take them to Ratnett anyway,' I said, realizing that no one had to call the coppers.

'And?' asked my mum.

'Well, think about it, Mum. If they know where Ratnett is, then we don't have to tell them, do we?'

'I man a try to tell yuh de same t'ing,' said Nanny, exasperated.

My mum considered our argument for a moment, realizing that we were right. There was no point in telling the police about Ronnie. They would find out anyway. If anything, I wanted to call Ronnie and warn him about the police. I didn't make the mistake of voicing my opinion, however – the mood my mum was in. I was more than happy to let her realize that we didn't have to get Nanny into grief with his friend. And realize she did.

'OK, I see your point,' she conceded. 'You know, sometimes it's like talking to a double act, talking to you two.'

I smiled at her. 'Like father, like son,' I said. I swear she had to hold back a tear.

I heard the back gate open and shut again, and went to the door. As I opened it, Zeus padded in, heading straight for his basket, followed by the others. I quickly filled them in on what was going on and immediately Della and Will were raring to go with Nanny. Nanny and my mum tried to tell them 'no' but it was no use.

'We'll wait for the police to deal wid Ratnett,' Della said, looking at me and Will. 'We won't even go anywhere close to the action – honest. I jus' wanna be out there when they find Jas – make sure he's all right.'

My mum sighed. 'Well, Ellie is definitely not going,' she told us. 'She's been through enough already.'

Ellie looked relieved at my mum's words. 'I'll stay and man the phones,' she said, looking enquiringly at me. 'Then I can text you if anything happens here you need to know about.'

I smiled at her and nodded. 'That's a good idea, Ellie – someone needs to keep us all up to speed.'

Ellie beamed at me.

I looked at my mum again, expecting her to put up resistance but she just nodded and then told us to be careful. 'Leave the criminals to the police,' she told us. 'Just make sure that Jas is OK.'

'It always best to leave de t'ief to de police,' agreed Nanny.

'Just keep the kids out of danger, Nanny.'

Nanny nodded.

I looked at Ellie, who was still smiling, walked over and gave her a kiss on her forehead. Then I did the same with my mum before turning to Nanny, Della and Will. 'Well, what are we waiting for? Let's make a move!'

thirty-six:

thursday, 1.30 a.m.

As soon as we hit the street Nanny got out his brick and called Ronnie Maddix, arranging to meet him down an alley that ran behind the church. The alley was a favourite spot for working girls whose punters didn't have cars or other places to go to – a local landmark, if you like. As soon as Nanny put his phone away we started to jog towards the crossroads where the church stood, reaching the meeting point in five minutes or so.

The junction had its usual night-time traffic and no one paid much attention to the dread and the youths jogging in their midst beyond a fleeting glance of recognition or interest. Further away the night air was filled with the wail of an ambulance siren, a blast from a passing police car and, somewhere, a scream, followed by yelling and then silence.

We made our way into the church grounds, a girl of no more than fifteen – dressed like a lapdancer – telling us that Ronnie was waiting for us round the back. The churchyard was dark, the two streetlamps closest to it broken again. On purpose. I found it hard to know where I was stepping in the darkness, glad that I had on trainers with a thick sole, just in case I stood on an upturned hypo or a used condom. Nanny rounded the wall into the alley, the rest of us right behind him, and we made our way down past the back of the church.

About halfway down Ronnie appeared in front of us. To this day I couldn't tell you where he came from. There was nowhere he could have been hidden – no bins or walls to shield him from us. He just came out of the darkness, scaring the shit out of me.

Nanny didn't even flinch. 'Yes, Ronnie,' he said, holding out a fist which Ronnie touched with his own.

'Nanny,' he said before looking to me. 'And his little crew.' He laughed.

'So wha' 'appen?' asked Nanny, ignoring Ronnie's jibe, nodding in the direction of the street.

'Got two girls out front watching things for me.'

Nanny noticed a red vinyl bag sitting on the floor. He pointed at it, looking at me. I was as puzzled as he was and shrugged my shoulders. 'What's in that?' I asked.

'Money,' replied Ronnie, smiling. 'Honey for the trap.'

'What trap?' Nanny and me spoke in unison. We didn't have a clue what Ronnie was on about.

Ronnie grinned this time, like a kid with the best new toy at Christmas. Then he outlined his plan to get Jas out. As he spoke I wondered how long it would be before DI Elliot turned up and whether I should warn Ronnie of her impending arrival. Once I'd heard the 'plan', I hoped she would show before he put it into action. The plan was all over the shop, and that was me being kind. Five minutes later I realized that my hoping was in vain and I cussed DI Elliot and the police under my breath as

Nanny and Ronnie made for the front of the church, the rest of us bringing up the rear.

'So which one is he in?' asked Della, nodding at the row of houses opposite the churchyard.

Ronnie raised his eyebrows at her and then looked at Nanny, giving *him* a reply to her question, making Della's eyes blaze with anger. 'It's hard to say,' he told Nanny. 'The whole block is joined up like an effing rabbit warren. The crackheads have knocked the bastard walls through and everything. Right little community they've got going. Could be he's anywhere in there.'

Will looked at me and Della and then swore.

'Is you actually sure dem in deh?' asked Nanny after telling Will to cool it.

'Yeah – one of the girls saw Ratnett go in. Apparently he's been using the place as a second headquarters – one his bosses don't know about.'

'What about the rockheads?' I asked.

'They've been moved on somewhere else,' laughed Ronnie. 'Probably by our friend Busta.'

The young girl who was standing just inside the churchyard approached and told Ronnie that the coast was clear. She pointed at a window two floors up on a house across the road. The house was on the corner of the main road and a side street called Seymour Road. There was a front door onto the main road but Ronnie told us that we were going in by an entrance in Seymour Road. The row of houses to which Ratnett's hideaway belonged had an alley running behind it, just like the ones on our street, and I asked Ronnie if we would be better going in via the back.

Ronnie shook his head. 'Nah. The entrance in

Seymour is better. The house used to be a knocking shop called Liberty's and the side-street entrance was the way in.'

'But surely Ratnett will know about it?' I asked.

Ronnie shook his head again. 'It ain't been used as an entrance for years,' he said. 'One of the girls told me about it.'

'So how are we supposed to get it open?' asked Della.

'It's already open, sweetheart. One of the girls checked it out.' Ronnie grinned at her, looking her up and down.

'And it gets us to the floor Jas is on?' asked Will.

'Yeah, through the door there's a flight of stairs. There's a fire door at the top. Past that door you're into a corridor, with about four rooms off it.'

'And you know which one Ratnett is in?' I said, beginning to feel anxious. Surely he'd hear us coming? Or see us?

'Yeah, kind of,' smiled Ronnie.

'Kind of? What de raas does that mean nuh, man?' Nanny gave his friend a puzzled look.

'Chill out, Nanny. The place is empty. It's a disused crack den.'

'Oh well, that's all right then,' I said, not caring whether Ronnie might take offence at my sarcasm. He just ignored me.

'Well, what we waitin' for?' urged Della.

'We just gonna walk right in?' asked Nanny, holding Della back by her arm, a stern look calming her down slightly. She was up for it.

'Yeah,' said Ronnie. 'He won't be expecting that – will he?' Gripping the red bag, he set off across the road and into the side street. We followed close behind. I wondered

215

what Ronnie was on. Some *plan*. As we approached the door, I started to get a bad feeling, worried that Ratnett would hear us. Scared that he might hurt Jas. Where were the effing police? As we went through the side door and onto a dark, smelly wooden fire escape, I started praying that DI Elliot would show up soon. My heart started pumping fast and sweat broke out on my forehead . . .

thirty-seven:

thursday, 2 a.m.

We climbed the stairs slowly, trying not to make any noise. It was an impossible task because the stairs were old, the wood rotten and flaking away underneath our feet. Halfway up I felt a step give and I fell forwards, cracking my head against the steps above. The jolting pain made my eyes water and for a moment I thought I was going to black out, but as I stood up I tried to steady myself, shaking my head.

Nanny turned and put his hand on my shoulder, whispering, 'Yuh all right, Billy?'

'Yeah,' I whispered back, feeling foolish.

Ronnie was standing in front of the fire door, trying to pull it open, but having no luck. It was stuck fast. He turned to Nanny.

'Bloody thing in't movin',' he whispered.

'So is how we gonna get inside?' asked Nanny.

Ronnie smiled and went inside his long, leather coat, pulling out a short crowbar. 'We'll use this,' he said, brandishing the tool and smiling at us.

'You just happened to have that on you?' Della asked out loud before realizing her mistake and lowering her voice.

'What else you got in there, Ronnie – chainsaw?' Will looked at me, his eyes asking why we were relying on this nutter.

Ronnie didn't notice. 'Nah, but it might be a good idea for the future,' he replied, still smiling.

'So why have you got a crowbar?' I insisted, wanting to know why he was carrying it. He wedged one end of it into the gap between the door and the frame, splintering the wood.

'In my game, you need a bit of protection,' he answered, as he leant his full weight into the tool, cracking more wood.

'Ssh,' whispered Della.

Ronnie looked at her like she was mad. 'Whaddya' mean "ssh"? You try an' get it open without making no noise.'

'Just open the raas ting,' said Nanny, giving Della a look that told her to shut up. She did.

Ronnie worked on at the door, pulling out small splinters of wood before a larger piece of the frame fell away. The door moved outwards from its resting place by thirty centimetres or so, its base scraping against the wooden floor, leaving a gap just big enough for me or Della to squeeze through but way too small for Nanny, Will or Ronnie. As Ronnie eased the door back some more, I beat Della though the gap, finding myself in a dark corridor. Pushing the door from the inside, I helped force it open some more, enough to allow the others through.

The smell in the corridor nearly made me throw up. It was damp and musty smelling, and somewhere there were rats or mice, possibly cat shit. I put my hand to my mouth and looked at Nanny, shrugging. He whispered for me to stay quiet and pointed down the corridor. Out of the gloom, we could make out about six doors, three on each side of the corridor. At the very end was a glass door, through which I could just make out a banister. The last door on the right had a light coming from it. Nanny looked at Ronnie, who nodded.

'That's gotta be where he's holding the kid,' said Ronnie in a whisper.

He gestured towards the door with his head and then started down the corridor, as much on tiptoe as a man of his height and weight could manage. For some reason, in the middle of all my nervousness, the image of a hippo in a tutu came to mind and I nearly burst out laughing, holding back at the last second. Luckily.

We followed Ronnie down the narrow corridor, which can't have been more than eight metres long. Nanny tried the first door on the right but it was locked shut. Will tried it again and it still didn't budge. There was a lock at the top and one about midway down, by the doorknob. The second door was pretty much the same so none of us attempted to open it.

As we reached the third one, the one with the light showing underneath the door, Ronnie held up his hand, putting the money down and motioning for us to stop. We did. He turned and handed Will the crowbar he had been carrying, then pulled a baseball bat from his coat and handed that to Nanny, who just smiled and shook his head. Turning to Della and me, he whispered that we should hang back. Della began to argue. Began to, but then he picked up the bag again – and produced a gun.

My heart took a bungee jump down into my bowels

and then back up into my throat. I looked at Nanny, my eyes wide. Nanny put a finger to his lips and then pulled Ronnie by the arm, pointing to the gun as Ronnie looked up. Ronnie smiled. *Smiled!* He was standing in the middle of a dark corridor, holding a gun, about to face a potential killer *and* policeman, and all he could do was smile. That was when I worked out that my mum and everyone else had been right. Ronnie really was as mad as everyone said and we *should* have called the police. My heart was racing by then and I got an urge to just turn round and go home, but the thought of Jas holed up in that smelly building stopped me. Ronnie had his own problem with the crooked copper, Ratnett. All I cared about was getting Jas out of there. And fast.

Ronnie tried the last door, slowly. The doorknob turned a little and then stopped. He tried harder and it began to turn again. There was a click from inside the mechanism and then the door opened, creaking and groaning. The light from inside the room flooded into the corridor and from nowhere a ginger tom cat that I kept on seeing around the neighbourhood wailed and ran out of the room and down the corridor to the fire escape. Della jerked backwards, startled, and bumped into me, neither of us noticing one of the doors behind us, to the left, open slightly. Ronnie edged into the room – gun first, money in the other hand, followed by Nanny and Will. I braced myself for the sound of gunfire or shouting but nothing happened. Instead the three of them entered the room untroubled. Della and me followed slowly.

Jas was sitting, tied to a chair, by a bricked-up window. Flashes of Ellie in the same predicament flooded back and I got a sense of déjà vu. By Jas's chair was a roll of masking tape and a glass of water that had been there a while, tiny bubbles floating inside the glass. Nanny and me rushed to untie Jas; Ronnie just walked over to the table and, putting his gun and bag down, dipped a finger into some powder residue, tasting it.

'Man,' he said, running his tongue along his gums. 'This is some serious shit.'

Underneath the table he found an Asda carrier bag. He emptied it out and three small balls of white powder, wrapped in cellophane, fell to the floor. Ronnie picked one up, and taking a knife from his pocket he slit the plastic and dipped the blade into the powder. He looked at it closely and then snorted it from the blade, shaking his head as he did so. He smiled. 'Tut tut,' he said, shaking his head again. 'What a silly place to leave a stash.'

No one was facing the door. The only person who could see the door was Jas and his eyes were about to pop out of his head. With Ronnie busy having an affair with someone else's narcotics, and the rest of us trying to untie all the tape round Jas's mouth, only Jas himself saw someone edge through the door, gun in hand. The voice from behind caught us all by surprise.

'TURN AROUND! SLOWLY!'

I looked at Nanny, who shrugged and then mouthed a few obscenities. We all turned slowly, finding Ratnett standing in the doorway, holding a gun. Ronnie was still bent over the table and instead of turning he tried to reach his own gun.

'LEAVE IT!' shouted Ratnett, aiming in Ronnie's direction.

'OK! OK!' Ronnie replied, turning to see Ratnett. 'Ah, Mr Ratnett,' he said, smiling like a maniac.

'Shut up and get over there with the rest of them!'

Ratnett gestured with the gun towards us. My heart did another bungee jump, but Nanny didn't even flinch. His eyes were set hard, staring straight at Ratnett. Will moved slowly in front of Della, like a protective wall. Ronnie grinned like an idiot and walked over to us.

Ratnett edged closer, all the while keeping his gun levelled at Ronnie's face. He eyed us all, one by one, before addressing Ronnie. 'Is this the best you could come up with?' he asked. 'A few niggers and half a Paki?'

'Times are hard,' replied Ronnie, smiling still.

I shot him an angry look but he just winked, gesturing with his eyes towards the gun on the table. I looked away.

'Well,' laughed Ratnett. 'They just got harder.'

And with that he smashed the butt of the gun in Ronnie's face, sending him falling backwards. He turned to Della and smiled. 'You – get your pretty self over here!'

Will almost lunged for Ratnett but the gun in his face told him to stop.

'Don't get clever, boy. No girl is worth dying over.'

I panicked, not knowing what to do. Nanny spoke up. 'Yuh nuh need de gal,' he said quietly.

Ratnett sneered. 'What I do and don't need is my business, Rastaman!' he said, snarling almost, spitting out the last word like it was dirt.

'It's all right,' said Della, surprising us all. 'I'll do what he says.'

I wanted to tell her 'no', to hold her back, but she just walked over to Ratnett calmly, showing no fear. Police sirens wailed in the distance. I looked up at Ratnett, wondering where DI Elliot had got to. Hoping, praying that she was outside with the rest of the police force . . .

thirty-eight:

thursday, 2.30 a.m.

'You in't gettin' away, Ratnett,' said Ronnie, spitting blood onto the bare floorboards.

'No?' he replied, sneering at Ronnie, and trying to hold Della still as she struggled in his one-armed grip.

'No,' I said, looking up at him.

He'd made us sit down on the floor – hands underneath us. Jas was still sitting in the chair, half untied, his eyes running from us to Ratnett and Della; to the gun on the table and back again. He looked wired and I began to wonder whether Ratnett had doped him up too, like Busta had with Sally.

'And what would you know about it?' Ratnett asked me.

'More than you, Babylon,' I said, looking away.

Ratnett held Della even tighter, around her midsection. 'What exactly?' he asked.

The glare that Nanny gave me told me to shut up. 'Nothing,' I said defiantly, looking at the policeman.

'Don't be a clever little shit,' warned Ratnett. 'You won't like the trouble you could get into.'

'Why yuh nah just let the girl go, man?' said Nanny. 'Ain't nuttin' she got dat yuh wan' anyway.'

Ratnett smiled. 'You wanna say that in English, dread?'

'You don't need her. Let her go.'

Ratnett sneered again and then moved his hand so that he had Della by her breasts. She struggled – trying to get away – but it was no use. I could see tears of anger welling in her eyes. Ratnett held her in the same way for a few more moments before moving his hands. I looked at him in disgust, wanting to tear his head from his shoulders. He was dead for that move.

'What I *need* is my money. And these kids have got it.'

'No they ain't,' said Ronnie. 'Yer boy – Busta – he ripped you off. The kids didn't have the second bag. Busta did.'

Ratnett looked at Ronnie, easing his hold on Della ever so slightly. 'Yeah? Well, I'll deal with him later,' he said, before eyeing the red bag that Ronnie had brought with him. 'So what's in that?' he asked.

Ronnie looked towards the red bag. 'It's the same amount of money that Busta nicked from you,' he said.

'What – you were just going to give me money, Maddix? Now, why would you want to settle Busta's debt?' asked Ratnett.

'In return for lettin' the kids off,' answered Ronnie. '*And* as part of a little deal.'

Will and I looked at Nanny, who shrugged. He knew as much as we did. 'What deal?' I said, looking at Ronnie.

'Shut up, kid.' He gave me a death stare. I shut my mouth.

'Well?' asked an impatient Ratnett. 'What deal?'

Della struggled a little more and Ratnett wasn't paying as much attention to his hold over her as he was to Ronnie's words.

'Simple,' explained Ronnie. 'You get all yer money back *plus* a cut of my profits, but only if you leave the dealers and the street trade to me.'

I couldn't believe it. Ronnie didn't give a shit about Jas or the rest of us. It was all about his business. His profits. Man, I felt stupid. I sat there in shock, anger welling up inside of me. Anger at being duped by Ronnie. Anger at not listening to my mum. But mainly anger at the fact that I was shocked by Ronnie's actions. I should have known that he was only here for himself. I turned to Nanny but he avoided my stare. Instead, he was focusing on Ronnie, trying, I think, to work out what Ronnie was up to. Whether he was being serious or just bluffing Ratnett – trying to get his guard down.

'You want me to let you have *everything*?' asked Ratnett.

'Yeah,' smiled Ronnie.

'But I don't *need* you,' he replied. 'I've already got my own people out there – dealing and collecting. Where do *you* come in?'

Ronnie thought for a minute as Della looked at me, trying to tell me something with her eyes.

'That's easy too. I *let* your crews carry on selling – if *you* agree. And if you don't – well then, your main men might have to go on a little trip. Out of town.'

'You're threatening *me*?' asked Ratnett, incredulous. '*I'm* the one holding the *gun*. Why don't I just kill you all – that way I get the lot.'

'Like you did Claire?' I said angrily.

'Shut up, kid. I'm not telling you a third time.'

'Oh go f—'

'You see – that's what my deal is all about,' said Ronnie, shifting his hands so that they were now by his side. Ratnett didn't notice. Ronnie carried on talking. 'You don't need to get your hands dirty, Mr Ratnett. You just leave all of that to me.'

'I don't *need* you – I just told you that.'

'Think about it,' insisted Ronnie. 'No more having to deal with all those bloody monkeys and that. No more having to take care of little problems – like the tart that grassed up your boy, Busta.'

'How'd you know about that?' asked Ratnett, startled and increasingly unable to hold Della still.

'How do I *know* anything, Mr Ratnett? Come on – I run this city – in't nothing happens without my knowledge.'

'You don't run anything, Ronnie,' sneered Ratnett. 'You *used* to . . .'

Ronnie shifted some more and from behind where I sat, Jas shifted in his chair, the creaking wood giving him away. Ratnett glanced at him and then turned back to Ronnie. Will began to edge towards me.

'Now, sit still all of you while I collect my money and my drugs,' ordered Ratnett. He looked at me. 'You stupid bastards. You could have just left the money alone. None of this would have happened then, would it? That tart would still be . . . Well, let's just say she'd still be selling her bits to anyone with a tenner to spare. And your mate there wouldn't have had to drink GBH like some date-rape bitch . . .'

I glared at him, willing him dead with the power of my thoughts. All in vain.

'. . . and as for this beautiful young girl . . . what can I say? She certainly doesn't mind a bit of rough, now does she . . . ?' He let his hands grope Della again.

The way he was touching Della set off an explosion of rage in my head. I leapt from my position on the floor, up at his neck, my hands grabbing his stubbly throat and squeezing. At the same time Della stamped down on his shin and foot. My vision blurred red as the blood smashed its way through my brain like a river bursting its banks, and I used all my weight to push Ratnett towards the table. The shock of such a sudden attack sent Ratnett backwards and he crashed onto the table, with me holding onto him – breaking the table in two.

Della managed to wriggle free as the gun went off, sending a bullet ricocheting around the room. The others ducked for cover. Ratnett tried to push me off with one hand, as he attempted to aim his gun with the other, but Della stamped on his arm and he let out a yelp of pain as the bones snapped like twigs. Suddenly he was pulled off me and Nanny was helping me to my feet. I cleared my head in time to see Ronnie and Della set about Ratnett with blow after blow. Will grabbed Della and pulled her away, telling her to calm down. Ronnie just carried on – grunting with the effort. Ratnett crumpled on the floor, out cold.

Will and Della then finished untying Jas, Nanny shouting at us to hurry and get out. His words were muffled. I couldn't hear a thing. My ears had popped and my nostrils were burning with the smell of gunshot. I looked at Ronnie, who smiled his sardonic smile and then picked up his bag of money again. Into it he put both guns, the wrapped cocaine, baseball bat and crowbar. Will grabbed Della, who was sobbing with shock, and led her out, leaving Jas to me. I went to follow them but then stopped to face Ronnie.

'You would have just let him go, wouldn't you?' I said. 'If that bastard had taken your deal.' My voice sounded strange to my own ears – like it was in slow motion or something. Spoken through water. And then my ears popped again.

Nanny walked over, supporting Jas. 'Yeah, Ronnie,' he said. 'What was all a dat shit 'bout a deal, man?'

'Relax Norris – it was just business. You're all off the hook, and between your evidence and this place, Ratnett's up shit creek. That leaves a nice hole in the market. Someone will take over. Might as well be me, my dread. Anyway, forget that – I'm taking our friend Mr Ratnett with me. We're gonna have a little talk about things and then I'm gonna ask him to record a little confession . . .'

'What if he doesn't?' I said.

'Oh, he will,' laughed Ronnie. 'Trust me.' He hoisted Ratnett over one shoulder as if he were bag of potatoes or something. I looked at him and he smiled. 'See yer around, kid,' he said. 'And don't worry about Busta – that nonce is getting what he deserves.'

'But he might mention you,' I said.

'Doubt it – but even if he does – I was never here, was I?' He grinned at me.

'Nice one, Ronnie,' I replied. 'See you around.'

'Yeah, you probably will. Say hello to yer old man for me,' he said.

'You what . . . ?' I asked, wondering what the hell he was talking about, but he didn't reply, disappearing down the back stairs and out onto Seymour Road.

Will and Della were waiting in the corridor and Jas leaned against me as I helped him out to join them. He was stoned out of his mind, his eyes opening wide for a few moments and then drooping shut. He was mumbling to himself. 'Gonna kill him, guy. Innit? Mess with me . . . man gwan get knock out, y'know . . .'

I stifled a laugh. He sounded like Prince Naseem.

A banging noise from the front entrance to the house, barely *seconds* later, announced DI Elliot's arrival. Talk about timing – it was as though Ronnie could *smell* the arrival of coppers. The front door sounded as though it were being smashed down and then the sound of heavy footsteps approached closer and closer.

'So what do we tell her this time?' I asked Nanny as the police came round the corner.

'Listen,' whispered Nanny urgently. 'We tell dem everyting wha' happen. Jus' don't mention Ronnie, see?'

'But what about Ratnett?' asked Will.

'Tell her him run away,' he replied.

Just then DI Elliot came out of the side entrance with two other coppers. She looked stunned to see us all standing there with Jas, who was still doing his Prince Naseem act.

'What the bloody hell are you doing here?' she demanded.

I looked at Nanny. 'You tell her,' I said.

Nanny smiled. 'Nah, man – I an' I nuh deal wid Babylon.' He grinned. 'Tell her yuh raasclaat self, Sleepy.'

Elliot looked ready to explode. '*Well?*' she asked, glaring at me.

Jas answered. '. . . Wha'? Hold *me* prisoner man? Man's getting *knocked* the *fuck* out — you gets me?'

I started to laugh.

thirty-nine:

later

And that's pretty much how it all ended. DI Elliot spent a week interviewing all of us, every day. She wanted to know about the bullet they'd found in the room, and what had happened to Ratnett. Whether there had been anyone else there that night. How we had known about the hideaway. The cocaine powder on the floor, the broken table, the fire escape — everything. We told her the same story, all of us. An anonymous phone call had tipped us off about Jas's whereabouts — *another* young girl, yes — and she hadn't given us her name, no. We had gone to the house, found the side entrance open and been told by a youth on a bike that some man had just legged it out of there, brandishing a gun.

Elliot asked for a description of the lad on the bike and she got one. Average height, normal build, black lad — could have been Asian — wearing a baseball cap, baggy jeans and a hooded top. No other distinguishing features. It could have described most of the young males in the ghetto — and that was the point.

'And there was definitely no one else present?' she'd asked me.

'Nah,' I'd said to her.

'Just your friend – tied up and alone?'

'Yeah. Looked like someone had been in a fight – there was a broken table, a few spots of blood on the floor. But no other person.'

DI Elliot had the blood matched and DNA-tested and it turned out that she had two different samples. One belonged to Ratnett and the other one was unknown. But it proved that someone else had been in that room. She put that to me during my last interview but I just shrugged.

'Might be that there was someone else,' I said, pausing to see her get all excited, thinking I was going to add more to my previous statements. She'd have had a long wait. 'Yeah, maybe there was,' I continued. 'But they must have gone before we arrived because when we got up there we just found a lot of mess and an incoherent Jas.'

That seemed to stall her questions and eventually she let us leave for the last time. As we stood outside waiting for my mum to pick us up, Elliot came out to join us.

'You know – not a lot of this makes sense,' she said, not looking at me but out at the traffic passing by on the ring road.

'What doesn't?' I asked innocently.

'It's just all too convenient.'

I looked at her and smiled. 'Sometimes things just happen that way. Have you found Ratnett yet?'

'No – but we're still looking. Won't be long.'

'Good,' I replied.

'Love to know who the other sample of blood belongs too.'

'Well, haven't you got a database that you can check

it against?' Della asked, guessing that they wouldn't find a match. Ronnie's last brush with the law had been years before they had started taking DNA samples as standard procedure – or so Nanny had told us.

'The person who left the blood isn't on the national system. Yet.' She turned to face us all, smiling. 'Let's hope I don't see you and your friends again too soon,' she added.

It was my turn to smile. 'You never know, DI Elliot. You just *never* know.'

'Man, I can't believe that we conned the Babylon like that!' laughed Della a few days later.

We were all in my bedroom, gathered around, talking about everything that had happened. Jas was back to his old self again after spending a few days in hospital. He had been our saviour as far as duping the police had gone. When they found us, Jas was taken straight to the hospital, his bloodstream full of a date-rape drug called GBH. They kept him there, and because he was so out of his head the police got little sense from him. When they did try and question him, they got a strange dope story about how he had been flying with his mates over the city – not in a plane, but with wings, like a bird. The next thing he remembered was that he was in a room with Prince Naseem Hamed, and the boxer was trying to spar with him. 'He was tryin' to knock me down, innit? So I jus' box him a lick and that.'

After that he told them that three men had broken into the room and Prince Naseem had vanished. He had no idea who the men were but there were definitely three. As for Ratnett, he remembered *him*. Ratnett had held a gun to his head, abducted him, threatened to kill him and then given him something to drink.

'Geezer smelt wack, y'know – like he'd not had a shower for a year. Rank, man, rank. Dutty Babylon.'

Della was still talking. 'That fool – fool bwoi Ratnett best not let me get to him first.'

'Is what you gonna do?' laughed Will.

Della snarled at him. 'Plenty, William. Plenty,' she replied.

'Hey, sister – I've told you – nuh bother call me William.'

'Wha'? You would rather I call you Willy? 'Cos that's yer choice, bwoi.'

Will scowled at her but she just ignored him – as usual.

'So didn't Ronnie Maddix tell you where he was taking the policeman?' asked Ellie.

'Oh yeah, Ellie,' answered Jas. 'Like he was gonna tell us. *Believe* dat, man.'

'Oh you nasty old people – I was only asking.'

'Ellie, please shut up and listen,' said Della. Ellie looked hurt and then pretended to sulk – until I reached over and pinched her arm.

'*Oww!*'

'Oh, Baby! Stop being so silly!' I said, grinning.

'Old man,' she replied, mumbling under her breath.

Della sighed and then continued to dis Ratnett. Will added something about how lucky Ratnett was that he hadn't managed to get hold of him.

'Oh yeah,' replied Jas, laughing. 'You was really the big hero. Check it – Big Willy. Super-hero.'

'At least I never got found off me head, chatting to Prince Naseem's ghost,' replied Will.

234

At that we all burst into laughter – apart, that is, from Jas, who sat where he was and looked sullen. 'Weren't funny, y'know,' he said, looking to Della for support. She blew him a kiss and then winked at Ellie, who started to giggle some more.

There was a knock at the door. I got up from where I was crouched on the floor, against my bed, and let Nanny in.

'Billy, yuh have a visitor,' he told me.

'Who?' I said.

Nanny just shrugged his shoulders. 'Maybe you bettah jus' check fe yuhself, man,' he replied.

I told the others that I'd be back in a minute and made my way downstairs. Nanny followed me and in the hallway he nodded towards the living room. 'In deh,' he told me, making his way to the kitchen. 'Lynden.'

I opened the living-room door and my heart nearly jumped out of my mouth. My dad.

He was sitting on the sofa, wearing a long, black leather coat, leather trousers and black boots. He had on a black shirt too, open necked, with gold chains hanging from his neck. Like an ageing Ragga star.

'Easy, Billy,' he said, grinning.

I caught my emotions, feeling ashamed of myself. Like I was letting down my mum and Nanny. 'All right,' I replied coldly.

'How's things, man?' he asked.

'Cool. Everything's cool, Dad.'

He grinned some more. 'And your mum – how's she doin'?'

'She's cool too,' I replied, noticing that he had a couple

of teeth missing. 'You been fighting?' I asked, pointing at his mouth.

He laughed, getting up gingerly. 'Ronnie said to say hello.'

'Ronnie?' I played dumb.

'Yeah. I work with him,' said my dad.

I looked him up and down, trying to remember the last time I had seen him. The trouble was that I had no idea when I had seen him last. It had been a long, long time ago. He hadn't changed that much. He looked away.

'Ronnie said to say thank you. He found the old nonce that kidnapped your girlfriend – Ellie, is it? Anyway the old pervert won't be touching no more girls from now on.'

I shook my head. 'She ain't my—' I began, but my dad interrupted.

'Whatever, Billy. Ronnie also told me to say that the copper you have in common will be giving himself up any day now.'

Ratnett.

'What did he do to him – and to the kidnapper?' I asked, knowing that I wouldn't get an answer.

'Come on, Billy, you know I can't tell you that,' he said.

'So why are you here?'

He walked towards me, his hand going into his coat pocket. I noticed that he was walking with a limp. From his pocket he produced an envelope – a brown, sealed one that looked padded. He threw it at me, smiling as I caught it one-handed.

'What's this?' I asked, looking at it.

'A present from Ronnie,' he said. He must have seen

the look on my face because he held up his hands. 'No strings, Billy. It's just a thank-you. He doesn't want anything for it.'

'How do you know?' I asked.

'Because it's from me too – me an' Ronnie are partners.'

I wanted to give the envelope back as much as I wanted to take it. My dad was in with Ronnie Maddix now – so I knew he was up to no good. How could I take a present from either of them? I knew what it was too – money. And judging by the weight of it – a lot of money.

'It's five grand,' he said, not even flinching. 'Yours.'

'I don't know what to say,' I told him.

'Say nothing. Just take it and do something with it. Your mum would say go to college or something.'

'OK.'

He walked right up to me and held out his hand. I shook it and then gave him a hug. I had wanted to do it as soon as I'd seen him but something had held me back. When I let him go there were tears in my eyes. He gave me his mobile number and told me to call him. We arranged to go out for a drink, me, my dad and my real dad, Nanny.

And then he left, limping out of the house and into a shiny black Audi A4. I watched him drive off and then made my way back upstairs. As I entered my room, I had a thought. I threw the envelope at Jas. 'You know that show up in Manchester?' I said to him.

'Yeah – what about it?' he replied, looking at the envelope.

'We're all going,' I said quietly, gesturing at the envelope.

Jas opened it and held up the contents. Will, Ellie and Della took in some breath before looking at me.

'Where'd that come from?' asked Della.

I smiled. 'Doesn't matter,' I told them. 'Best left alone.'

'Oh, stop being so mysterious, you old man,' said Ellie, grinning.

'Ellie . . . ?' we all said in unison.

She pouted at us and grinned. 'I *know* . . . I *know* – shut up . . .'

bali rai

(un)arranged marriage

Harry and Ranjit were waiting for me – waiting to take me to Derby, to a wedding. My wedding. A wedding that I hadn't asked for, that I didn't want. To a girl who I didn't know…

If they had bothered to open their eyes, they would have seen me: seventeen, angry, upset but determined – determined to do my own thing, to choose my own path in life…

Set partly in the UK and partly in the Punjab region of India, this is a fresh, bitingly perceptive and totally up-to-the-minute look at one young man's fight to free himself from family expectations and to be himself, free to dance to his own tune.

WINNER OF THREE
CHILDREN'S BOOK AWARDS

0552 547344

about the author

BALI RAI is a writer from Leicester. Sometimes he is young and exciting, but mostly he is too busy trying to get his next project in on time. As a Politics graduate, if he absolutely had to get a real job, he'd pick journalism. For now, he is happy to write although he quite misses working behind a bar. This is more than made up for, however, by the fact that he can now get out of bed when he likes, and that nice people keep on asking him to visit them in wonderful places all over Europe. He'd like to mention, too, that he isn't married, doesn't want to get married, and doesn't really want to work in Bollywood – although, judging by the photo, he may have no choice in the matter.

The Crew is his second book for Corgi Books. The first, *(un)arranged marriage*, appeared on a number of award shortlists and won the Angus Book Award, the Leicester Book of the Year Award and the Stockport Schools Award. He was also threatened on the radio by an old Punjabi woman with what appeared to be a sandal. He thinks it may have been his mum, but isn't too sure. Until he finds out, he'll carry on writing his next story and try to stay out of sight.